R.GOSCINNY - A.UDERZO

Asterix

ADVENTURE GAMES
ASTERIX AGAINST ALL ODDS

based on *Asterix and the Banquet*

Illustrated by Uderzo

HODDER AND STOUGHTON
LONDON SYDNEY AUCKLAND

British Library Cataloguing in Publication Data

A catalogue record for this book is available from the British Library

ISBN 0 340 54874 6

Text and illustrations copyright © Les Editions Albert René, Goscinny-Uderzo, 1992
Concept copyright © Stephen Thraves 1992
Compiled by Stephen Thraves

First published 1992

All rights reserved. No part of this publication may be reproduced or
transmitted in any form or by any means, electronically or mechanically,
including photocopying, recording, or any information storage and
retrieval system, without either prior permission in writing from the
publisher or a licence permitting restricted copying. In the United
Kingdom such licences are issued by the Copyright Licensing Agency,
90 Tottenham Court Road, London W1P 9HE.

The rights of Stephen Thraves to be identified as the author of the text
of this work and of Uderzo to be identified as the illustrator of this
work have been asserted by them in accordance with the Copyright,
Designs and Patents Act 1988.

Published by Hodder and Stoughton Children's Books,
a division of Hodder and Stoughton Ltd,
Mill Road, Dunton Green, Sevenoaks, Kent TN13 2YA

Photoset by Rowland Phototypesetting Ltd,
Bury St Edmunds, Suffolk

Printed in Great Britain by BPCC Hazells Ltd
Aylesbury, Bucks, England
Member of BPCC Ltd

You will doubtless already be acquainted with Asterix's many adventures and his numerous confrontations with the mighty Roman army. Time and time again, this cunning little Gaul has put their Roman noses out of joint!

But Asterix and his overgrown friend, Obelix, are now about to embark on a very *different* type of adventure. It's different because this time they are putting their fate entirely in YOUR hands. It is YOU who must decide which routes they follow . . . what risks they take.

Unless you are very lucky, it's unlikely that you will lead them to the end of this perilous adventure on your very first attempt. But the more times you play, the more experienced you will become at choosing the safest routes and options – and the further you'll advance them on the adventure.

Even when you *have* finally led our heroes right to the end of the adventure, you'll still want to play the game again.

For there's another challenge: not just to reach the end of the adventure but to reach it with as little magic potion consumed as possible! Each time you play, you should try and better this score, aiming eventually for *no magic potion consumed at all*. Only then can you rightly consider yourself as cunning as the little Gaul himself!

THE ADVENTURE BEGINS . . .

The year is 50 BC. Gaul is entirely occupied by the Romans. Well, not entirely . . . Asterix's little village in the north-west corner still manages to hold out against the invaders. The secret of their success lies in the magic potion brewed by an ancient Druid, Getafix, which bestows a superhuman strength.

But how successful would this little band of independent Gauls be *outside* their village? This is the impertinent question put to them one day by an artful Roman centurion. 'You're just big frogs in a small pool!' he taunts the village's chief, Vitalstatistix. 'Your men wouldn't last very long in a much larger pool. I'm talking about all Gaul. You'd be no more than tadpoles out there!'

'Tadpoles, eh?' Vitalstatistix replies furiously. 'We'll see about tadpoles! I'll wager that my two most formidable warriors, Asterix and Obelix, can make their way right round occupied Gaul!'

'Oh yes!' mocks the centurion. 'And how do I know that they won't cheat? How do I know that they won't just hide in a nearby forest for a few weeks and *pretend* that they have travelled the whole country?'

'Because we'll take a large shopping bag with us!' Asterix joins in, suddenly having a brainwave. 'And we'll put in that shopping bag the food or drink each town along the route is famous for. When we get back we'll invite you to a banquet of all these foods. All *you* will be eating, though, is humble pie!'

So the wager is agreed upon, the challenge is set.

Knowing that the two Gauls are going to meet hundreds of Romans on their journey, Getafix gives Asterix a gourd of special strength magic potion. 'None for you, of course, Obelix,' the Druid forbids him, 'because you fell into a cauldron of my magic potion as a baby and that will last you for life!'

Getafix has another word of warning for Asterix's overgrown friend. 'And on this occasion, I don't want you fighting any more Romans than is absolutely necessary. The most important thing is that you both just *complete* the journey. The honour of our village is at stake!'

WHAT TO DO

To guide our heroes on this mission, you start at PARAGRAPH ONE overleaf and then follow the instructions to other paragraphs. You will often be given a choice of paragraphs to go to and the skill of the game is to try to select the options that won't cause Asterix to use up too much of his magic potion.

The gourd of magic potion that Getafix gave him contains *eight* measures in all, so turn the dial on the MAGIC POTION COUNTER so that 8 shows through the window. Every time Asterix drinks or spills a measure of his potion, you must turn the dial to reduce this score.

If the number on the COUNTER falls to 0 it means that Asterix has completely run out of magic potion and he must immediately abandon his journey. If you want him to make another attempt at the challenge, you must start the game all over again, beginning at PARAGRAPH ONE.

Asterix is most likely to use up some of his magic potion whenever the Gauls have a fight with the Romans – and so you should try to avoid these confrontations. At the very least, you should try to avoid confrontations with a *large number* of Romans. The more Romans the Gauls have to fight, the more chance there is that Asterix's strength will be sapped . . . and so the more measures of magic potion he will have to drink to restore that strength.

Whenever you get the Gauls into a fight, you must throw the special dice to represent that fight. For instance, if the paragraph tells you that the Gauls are confronted by *seven* Roman patrols, you keep throwing the dice until they have knocked out these seven patrols. The Gauls knock out one patrol every time you roll a 'stunned soldier'.

If the 'gourd of magic potion' is rolled at any time during the fight, this means that Asterix's strength is flagging and he briefly has to break off from the fight to revive himself with a measure of potion. You may find that this occurs several times before the Gauls have knocked out the total number of Roman patrols and every measure of magic potion rolled must be deducted from the score on the MAGIC POTION COUNTER.

There are other occasions, apart from fights, when Asterix's magic potion could be diminished. He might spill some of it while taking flight, perhaps, or be forced to give some of it away. These misfortunes will tend to occur if, for example, Asterix can't prove to fellow Gauls that he isn't a spy . . . or he can't pay for his lodgings.

You can help him avoid these sort of tricky situations, however, if you lead him to one or more of the following useful ITEMS: a *coinbag*, a *password scroll* and a *sketchpad of allies*. These three special ITEMS are contained in the wallet but you can only make use of them if you manage to locate them during the adventure. Until that time the three cards must always be kept face down and out of play.

Remember: your ultimate aim is not just to guide Asterix to the end of the journey but to do this *with as little magic potion consumed as possible*. The higher the final score on your MAGIC POTION COUNTER, the better you have done!

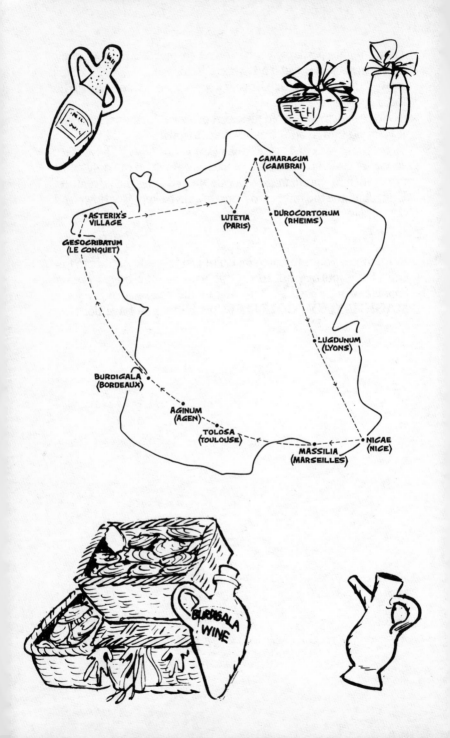

You are now ready to start this perilous journey. May the gods be with you!

'What a beautiful day it is and what beautiful countryside!' Asterix remarks happily as he and Obelix leave their village and head for the very first destination on their route. Obelix's little dog, Dogmatix, is also making the long journey but for the moment he is somewhere ahead of them or behind them, sniffing for rabbits in the bushes. 'Our first port of call is Lutetia, capital of Gaul,' Asterix says as he strides cheerfully along. 'Let's hope we reach it before that centurion alerts the occupying army that we're coming!' But the centurion's messengers are well ahead of the Gauls, galloping from one Roman garrison to the next. And early the next morning, two Roman contingents – one of five patrols, the other of eight – are advancing towards our heroes. They hide themselves in a wood only a few miles ahead of Asterix and Obelix, the five-patrol contingent lying in wait in one part of the wood and the eight-patrol contingent in another. 'We're coming to a wood,' Asterix announces breezily, totally unaware of these two traps. 'There appear to be three paths through it; one on its east side, one on its west, and one straight through the middle!'

Which path will you choose for them?

If path on east side	**go to 267**
If path in middle	**go to 206**
If path on west side	**go to 51**

2
THE GAULS
ARE CONFRONTED BY

ROMAN PATROLS HERE

Keep throwing the dice until the Gauls have knocked out this number of patrols. Any magic potions rolled before this total is reached must be deducted from the score on the MAGIC POTION COUNTER. When the Gauls have finished the fight, go to 27.

3

The Gauls have nearly reached Burdigala when they suddenly encounter a number of fallen trees. They completely block the river path. 'Never mind, Asterix,' Obelix tells him as he reads a sign in front of the trees. 'Look, it instructs us to follow one of three detour paths to Burdigala.' Asterix is very suspicious about the fallen trees, though. And even more suspicious about the detour paths! Peering into the distance, he sees that one of them leads towards a wood, one towards a narrow gap between two hills and one towards a huddle of cowsheds. Every one of these places, of course, would be ideal for an ambush!

Which detour path do you want them to take?

If path that leads through wood   **go to 97**
If path that leads towards two hills   **go to 66**
If path that leads towards cowsheds   **go to 245**

4

'Isn't the idea that vehicles are meant to *stop* at a roadblock?' one of the battered Romans asks another as he nurses his black eye. 'Well, I always took that to be the general idea,' the other replies through his thickened lips. 'I thought that was the point of us standing in a firm unbroken line and defiantly raising our spears!' The Gauls are by now far away from this debris, racing on towards Lugdunum. In a few more hours, they reach the maze-like streets of the town. 'I bet that's the fastest delivery they've ever had!' Asterix exclaims as they jump down from the post-cart and give their legs a much-needed stretch. *Go to 218.*

5

The captain refuses to believe Asterix though. 'Humbug!' he barks as he draws out his sword. Asterix immediately draws out his own sword but this time it is Obelix who does the restraining. 'No, he didn't mean to insult you,' he tells his friend. 'I think he just wants one of those little minty sweets himself!' Asterix lets out a long sigh. 'Why can't you get it right, Obelix?' he snaps. 'This time "humbug" really does mean "humbug"!' *Go to 248.*

6

'What a fine horse we've picked,' Asterix says as it gallops past one milestone after another. 'At this rate,' he adds, 'we should reach Camaracum in plenty of time for supper!' Even when it starts to rain, the horse is still able to keep up a reasonably good pace. 'Its horseshoes hold the road so well, don't they?' Asterix remarks, highly impressed. But Obelix's attention was lost from the moment Asterix had mentioned the word 'supper'. His mind is thinking about half a dozen or so roast boar with a little of the local stuffing. Just the smallest *spoonful* of stuffing, mind. He doesn't like to think of himself as greedy! *Go to 101.*

7
THE GAULS
ARE CONFRONTED BY

ROMAN PATROLS HERE

Keep throwing the dice until the Gauls have knocked out this number of patrols. Any magic potions rolled before this total is reached must be deducted from the score on the MAGIC POTION COUNTER. When the Gauls have finished the fight, go to 186.

'Come on, Obelix, we're in a hurry!' Asterix calls to his friend as he dusts off his hands and jumps back into the chariot. 'Why are you staring over the bridge? And why so anxiously?' he asks. Obelix tells him that he's worried that some of the Romans spluttering in the water down there might not be able to swim. 'Do you think we should go and fish them out?' he asks. Asterix isn't the slightest bit taken in by his friend's phoney concern, though. 'Now you know very well, Obelix, that swimming is part of every Roman's basic training,' he chides him. 'And *I* know very well that you want to fish them out just so that you can toss them back in again!' *Go to 137.*

'No, Nosepix isn't my name,' the shopkeeper answers suspiciously. 'Why do you ask?' His suspicion seems to prove that he *is* the local Resistance leader – but Asterix realises he has blown it now. He can't just try another name! He feels he ought to try to help his organisation, though. 'We must give you something for these bottles of wine,' he says as he pours a little of his magic potion into a goblet for him. 'Try some of this in return.' The shopkeeper asks if it has the same sort of kick as his fizzy wine. 'You could say that!' Asterix exclaims as he and Obelix now bid him goodbye.

Reduce MAGIC POTION by 1 measure. Go next to 261.

10

'Would you like a lift?' a passing cart-driver asks the Gauls as they are walking along this pleasant country road. 'I'm going as far as Durocortorum. I've got to deliver this barrel of wine there.' The trio gratefully accept his kind offer; Asterix climbing up alongside the driver while Obelix and Dogmatix squeeze in next to the barrel in the back of the cart. They all think they're in for a nice gentle ride but the cart-driver is not nearly as meek as he looks. He cracks his whip hard and has his poor horse galloping so fast that Asterix eventually insists that they must stop at an inn to rest it for a while. *Go to 215.*

11

'These long distance chariot journeys are really wearing me out,' Asterix sighs when they at last reach Nicae. 'Since we're still a little ahead of schedule,' he suggests, 'let's spend a few hours relaxing on the beach. I could do with a bit of sun!' So they immediately make their way to the sea-front. 'I've never seen so many people!' Asterix gasps as they arrive at the promenade. 'I wonder which part will be the least crowded. Do we head for the north end of the beach, the south end or just stay here in the very middle?'

What will you decide for them?

If head for north end	**go to 31**
If head for south end	**go to 118**
If remain where they are	**go to 146**

12

Enquiring at a tourist and invaders office, the Gauls find out that the quickest way to walk to Massilia is by crossing the mountains. They're not too high in this part and the mountain route is a lot more direct than the zigzagging road that follows the coastline. The free guide-book they're given shows that there are four scenic footpaths they can take. There's the 'deer path', the 'kestrel path', the 'myrtleberry path' and the 'blueberry path'. The guide-book tells of the various flora and fauna that can be found along each path. What it *doesn't* tell them, though, is that each path also has a contingent of Romans lying in wait for them!

Which path do you want them to take?

If 'deer path'	**go to 164**
If 'kestrel path'	**go to 289**
If 'myrtleberry path'	**go to 80**
If 'blueberry path'	**go to 178**

'Excuse me,' Asterix brazenly asks the shopkeeper, 'but are you the leader of the local Resistance here?' The shopkeeper instantly goes on the defensive, demanding why he wants to know. 'Are you a

Roman spy?' he asks, shaking. 'Call me by my correct name to prove that you're one of us!' Asterix is sure that the farmer said his name was either Freekix, Spongemix or Klunkklix. But for the life of him, he can't remember which!

If you have picked up the SKETCHPAD during the adventure, you may consult it here to find out the shopkeeper's name. If not, you'll have to guess which of the possibilities Asterix should give.

If you prefer FREEKIX   **go to 276**
If you prefer SPONGEMIX   **go to 210**
If you prefer KLUNKKLIX   **go to 61**

'No, my name isn't Spongemix,' the waiter replies irritably as Asterix plucks at his sleeve. 'Now perhaps you would kindly let me get on. Can't you see how many people there are here waiting to be served? It's like a madhouse, I tell you!' So Asterix seems to have no choice but to let the waiter go and he disappointedly returns his attention to his boar chop. Suddenly, though, a scream of 'SOLDIERS!' rings out above the manic chatter . . . *Go to 247.*

15
THE GAULS
ARE CONFRONTED BY

ROMAN PATROLS HERE

Keep throwing the dice until the Gauls have knocked out this number of patrols. Any magic potions rolled before this total is reached must be deducted from the score on the MAGIC POTION COUNTER. When the Gauls have finished the fight, go to 271.

16

Asterix again finds himself receiving a suffocating embrace. 'You're right again!' the farmer cries. 'And only Asterix himself could have known that piece of information! There weren't any Romans present when he received the manuscripts from Cleopatra. You must be Obelix, then?' The farmer is about to give his enormous body an embrace as well but then realises that his arms probably wouldn't reach round that far! 'Er . . . perhaps I should get straight on with these sketches,' he suggests tactfully, pulling the sketchpad from under his shirt and a stick of charcoal from behind his ear. The sketches are soon finished and Asterix gratefully tucks the pad into his belt as the farmer wishes them good luck on their quest.

You are now entitled to use the SKETCHPAD CARD. Go next to 227.

17

'There you are, the finest I have!' the owner says when the Gauls have asked for some bottles of fizzy wine in the shop with the yellow awning. 'Is it for a *very* special occasion?' he adds affably. 'I hope so because it doesn't come cheap, I'm afraid. That brand will cost you two gold coins a bottle.' Asterix does a quick calculation in his head (and Obelix a rather slower calculation). That works out at *six* gold coins (although Obelix makes it *five*) in all! This special fizzy wine is even more expensive than either of them were expecting!

If you have picked up the COINBAG during the adventure, you can use this to pay the shopkeeper. Rotate the disc to 'count out' the 6 gold coins – then go to the number that appears on the other side of the card. If you don't have the COINBAG, go to 140 instead.

18
THE GAULS
ARE CONFRONTED BY

ROMAN PATROLS HERE

Keep throwing the dice until the Gauls have knocked out this number of patrols. Any magic potions rolled before this total is reached must be deducted from the score on the MAGIC POTION COUNTER. When the Gauls have finished the fight, go to 88.

19

To pay for their passage, the ship's captain insists that the Gauls join the crew in swabbing the decks. For the whole of the first day of the voyage Asterix and Obelix are very grudging about this. But half-way through the second day they have reason to change their minds. A huge fleet of Roman galleys intercepts their ship! 'They're obviously looking for *us!*' Asterix whispers to his friend as a stern centurion comes on board, accompanied by a large contingent of soldiers. 'Just keep your head down and continue with your swabbing and hopefully they won't notice us!' *Go to 265.*

20

'Why have they tied up your arms and legs like that, Asterix?' an intrigued Obelix asks after the captain has ordered his crew to prepare the little Gaul for the keel-hauling. 'I think it's some sort of game,' Asterix replies, 'but just in case, perhaps you could give me a

quick swig of my magic potion. I'm a bit tied up at the moment!'
After a sombre rolling of the drums the keel-hauling commences. 'I
think the sharks must have got him, cap'n,' one of the crew
announces after Asterix has been hauled right down underneath
the ship. 'I can't feel any more tugging on the rope!' But suddenly
he does feel a tug. And so do all the other crew members trying to
pull Asterix up again. A tug so fierce that they all go flying over the
side of the boat themselves!

Reduce MAGIC POTION by 1 measure. Go next to 217.

21

'Well, what a cunning plan, I must say!' exclaims one battered
soldier in the devastated camp. But he's exclaiming it only to
himself because he's the single one there who hasn't been left
completely unconscious! 'Yes, so *cunning*!' he continues ironically.
'What we'll do, our smartypants centurion tells us, is turn the
signpost round: so instead of the Gauls strolling back to their village
they'll stroll right into our camp!' The soldier now crawls over to the
unconscious centurion and shouts in his ear. 'There was just one
thing wrong with the plan, sir,' he yells. 'It worked!' *Go to 263*.

Our heroes are about half-way to their next destination, Burdigala, when they encounter a large flooded area. It means that they have to turn their horses away from the river-bank and take a long detour. This detour path eventually brings them to a picturesque country village and they decide to stop off for a quick lunch. Their choice of inns is either The Cheese and Onion, The Ready Salted or The Smokey Boar. But the inns are not as *inn*ocent as they look. For, hiding in each inn, waiting for the Gauls, there's a contingent of Roman soldiers!

Which inn do you want the Gauls to enter?

> If The Cheese and Onion   **go to 46**
> If The Ready Salted   **go to 185**
> If The Smokey Boar   **go to 203**

23
THE GAULS
ARE CONFRONTED BY

ROMAN PATROLS HERE

Keep throwing the dice until the Gauls have knocked out this number of patrols. Any magic potions rolled before this total is reached must be deducted from the score on the MAGIC POTION COUNTER. When the Gauls have finished the fight, go to 160.

'What a relief it is to put Lutetia behind us!' Asterix exclaims as they at last reach the open road again and follow the signs for their next destination. It's the town of Camaracum in the top right corner of Gaul, just short of the Belgian border. The walk is likely to take them a good two days but, as luck would have it, they come across three unattended Roman chariots in the courtyard of a roadside inn. They decide to borrow one of them! What they don't realise, though, is that only one of the chariots is harnessed to a horse which is likely to make the whole journey!

Which chariot do you want them to take?

If chariot drawn by the brown horse	**go to 59**
If chariot drawn by the black horse	**go to 6**
If chariot drawn by the white horse	**go to 109**

Finally emerging from the wood, our heroes enter a cowfield. 'It's milking time,' Asterix remarks to his friend, noticing a farmer seated beneath one of the cows on a little stool. 'You'd better call Dogmatix to heel,' he warns. 'We don't want him chasing any of the cows or their milk will be turned to cheese. Then the farmer really will be cheesed off!' As they're passing quietly through the field, Asterix suggests that they check with the farmer that they are heading in the right direction for Lutetia. *Go to 229*.

26

'I thought we were stopping only for a tankard of goats' milk each!'
Asterix remarks as Obelix struggles with his tray of food towards an
empty table. Obelix completely polishes off one of his baked boar
before replying. He doesn't like to talk with his mouth full! 'Well, I
suddenly had this brilliant idea,' he says, licking his fingers. 'The
longer we sit here eating,' he explains, 'the more the traffic will have
died down!' ***Go to 168***.

27

'I don't suppose there's just *one more* Roman hiding anywhere?
Even a little one?' Obelix asks hopefully, as the farmer's hut lies in
ruins all about them. 'These fights are always over so quickly. I was
just beginning to warm up! What about under this bed?' Peering
under the crushed bed, he doesn't find any Romans but he *does* find
the quaking farmer. The farmer who betrayed them for a few gold
coins! 'I'm staying right where I am,' the wretch bleats at Obelix.
'You're much too big to squeeze under here and get me!' Obelix
may be too big . . . but Dogmatix isn't! Yapping and snarling, the
little dog quickly drives the farmer out from his refuge – and into
Obelix's eager hands. 'I'm getting a lot warmer now,' he says as he
gives the farmer a good shake. 'How about you?' ***Go to 129***.

'Sssh, keep your voices down!' the man in the boat whispers to them anxiously. 'How on earth did you know that my name was Chokkybix? Yes, of course, I know! You must be the famous Asterix and Obelix that I've heard so much about!' His whisper becomes even more furtive as he tells them that he is about to make a 'spear-running' (the ancient equivalent of gun-running) trip in the boat. 'The spears are all hidden under this canvas sheet,' he tells them, pointing to a long bumpy bundle at his feet. 'I'm delivering them to Resistance members who are hiding at various places further along the coast. I'll let them know that you're coming so they can try and nobble a few Roman contingents for you in advance!' *Go to 174*.

'When I'm not drawing milk I like to draw portraits,' the farmer explains. 'So I could do a quick sketch of all these Resistance contacts for you. But I insist on some sort of proof that you are who you say you are. We have heard tell that one of Asterix's most heroic feats was when he beat the Roman athletic champion at the Olympic Games. The champion tried to cheat by stealing some magic potion but Getafix had laced it with an extra ingredient that dyed his tongue. What colour was that dye?' Asterix desperately racks his brains. The problem is that he has accomplished so many heroic feats that he can't always remember the details!

Which colour would you suggest Asterix answers?

If you think blue	**go to 251**
If you think green	**go to 93**
If you think yellow	**go to 157**

30

While the Gauls are buying a basket of oysters at a quayside stall, Obelix foolishly puts down his shopping bag for a moment. When he turns round to pick it up again, he finds that it has gone. All their purchases for the banquet have been stolen! 'The thief must have run on to one of those three ships being loaded over there,' Asterix says as he desperately looks all round for him. 'There's nowhere else he could have gone. But *which* ship do we search?'

Which of the three ships will you choose for them?

If ship being loaded with baskets	**go to 41**
If ship being loaded with wine barrels	**go to 150**
If ship being loaded with crates	**go to 223**

The trio have just made themselves comfortable at the north end of the beach when a Gaul in a white overall approaches them, pushing a little cart across the sand. 'Iced goats' milk . . . iced goats' milk?' he starts to pester them. Asterix irritably tells the vendor to buzz off but Obelix is rather tempted by this strange food. 'I'll have a dozen large portions, please,' he says. 'No, you'd better make that just ten. They look as if they might melt quickly!' The vendor digs a scoop into the large bucket on his cart, transferring the icy dollops to wafer cornets. 'That will be twenty gold coins!' he tells them.

If you have picked up the COINBAG during the adventure, you can use this to pay the vendor. Rotate the disc to 'count out' the 20 gold coins – then go to the number that appears on the other side of the card. If you don't have the COINBAG, go to 110 instead.

32

'I thought *we* were meant to be ambushing *them*,' one of the dazed Romans grumbles to his partner as the Gauls leave them all in a heap behind them. 'Well, it's all these confusing alleys,' the partner replies, once the stars have cleared before his eyes. 'It makes it very difficult to tell. Give me the more conventional ambush, that's what I say. You know – the one where we hide behind some bushes at the side of an open road. It's always much clearer who's ambushing whom with those!' *Go to 218.*

33

'An amphora of goats' milk and two oxman's lunches, please,'
Asterix says to the innkeeper after he has casually stepped over all
the dazed Romans and made his way to the bar. 'What a charming
little place you have here,' he adds, making friendly conversation.
'Just the sort of peace and quiet that I like!' The innkeeper is too
stunned by what he has just witnessed to reply, however. He simply
gapes at Asterix. 'Oh, you sometimes get a little a fed up with all the
peace and quiet, do you?' Asterix continues, somewhat misin-
terpreting the expression. 'Yes, I suppose an out of the way place
like this does rather miss out on the action!' ***Go to 149***.

34

'Nosepix?' Asterix enquires politely as they approach the man
drying his hair. The man's large wife puts her hands to her hips,
scowling at them. 'My husband certainly *doesn't* pick his nose!' she
snaps. 'And, even if he does, what's it to do with you?' Asterix
realises that he has lost his chance. But he's absolutely convinced
now that this is the local Resistance leader. So he secretly pours a
little of his potion into the amphora of fizzy spa water (the ancient
equivalent of a bottle of lemonade) at the man's side. Even if he
doesn't need it to fend off the Romans, he could surely do with it to
fend off that fearsome wife!

Reduce MAGIC POTION by 1 measure. Go next to 241.

'I won our bet! I won our bet!' one of the dazed Romans boasts delightedly to his friend as the Gauls disappear into the distance. 'See? I told you that they would choose *our* path. You said they would take one of the others but I said it would be this one. That's twenty sestertii you owe me!' But it's going to be a little while before the friend can pay him the wager. He is even *more* dazed. In fact, he's completely unconscious! ***Go to 40.***

Obelix continues to look bewildered as Asterix uncorks his gourd of magic potion and pours a measure on to the ground for Dogmatix. 'There's our bull!' he chuckles as Dogmatix starts to snort and roar from the effect of the potion. The little dog then charges at the Roman, his steaming body pounding the quay. The terrified Roman quickly throws his cloak over his sword to form a matador's cloak but Dogmatix ploughs right through it and knocks him clean into the murky sea below!

Reduce MAGIC POTION by 1 measure. Go next to 174.

Obelix was right. As the trio enter the novelty shop (proprietor: Boxatrix), they just catch the Roman disappearing behind a large curtain at the back. He must be trying on a fancy dress costume for the orgy! The Gauls wait patiently for him to step out again, pretending to be looking at some of the practical jokes in the shop. Eventually, the Roman emerges again – dressed as a Greek goddess! Or is it him . . . because two others, one dressed as a senator and the other as a veiled belly-dancer, also emerge. What's worse, all three customers like their outfits so much that they decide to keep them on. So which one do the Gauls follow along the street *now*?

What will you decide for them?

If follow the Greek goddess   **go to 133**

If follow the senator   **go to 187**

If follow the veiled belly-dancer   **go to 58**

38

When the Roman barks at him that his password was wrong, Asterix decides just to play it cool. 'Well, I don't deny that I was only guessing,' he replies. 'I didn't say that we *were* from round here, did I? Yes, we *are* northerners – but so what? You people should be flattered that we've travelled so far for our holidays. Now perhaps you would move out of my sun so I can get on with my tanning!' The act convinces the Roman – but Asterix is just a bit *too* nonchalant. Pretending to be splashing a little bit of suntan lotion on to his arms, he suddenly realises that it's his magic potion he's wasting!

Reduce MAGIC POTION by 1 measure. Go next to 241.

39
THE GAULS
ARE CONFRONTED BY

ROMAN PATROLS HERE

Keep throwing the dice until the Gauls have knocked out this number of patrols. Any magic potions rolled before this total is reached must be deducted from the score on the MAGIC POTION COUNTER. When the Gauls have finished the fight, go to 165.

40
Our heroes finally reach Massilia and wander round the town's harbour. 'I don't suppose the speciality *here* is . . . ?' Obelix begins but Asterix again has to disappoint him. 'No, it's not wild boar, I'm afraid,' he tells him. 'It's fish stew. But quite delicious fish stew, I'm told. We'll ask that fisherman mending his nets over there where we can buy a pot of it.' *Go to 242.*

41

'Has anyone come on board carrying a large bag?' Asterix hurriedly asks the ship's captain when they have raced up the gangplank. 'Yes, they have,' the captain replies. 'A stranger with a large bag over his shoulder told me he wanted to join my crew!' The Gauls are delighted by this, eagerly asking where this man is. 'Scrubbing the poop deck,' the captain says, pointing behind them. 'At least he *was* a few moments ago . . .' he adds bewilderedly. The Gauls search all round for the thief but there's absolutely no sign of him. 'He must have jumped overboard when he saw us coming up the gangplank,' Asterix surmises. 'Never mind,' he continues as he joyfully spots their shopping bag on the poop deck, 'at least he was thoughtful enough not to take *this* with him!' *Go to 48*.

42

At last Asterix manages to free one of his wrists and he immediately reaches for his gourd of magic potion. 'I thought these Gauls were meant to be a real handful,' one of the Romans at the back of the contingent comments to his partner after the soldiers have turned the next corner. 'It's just Gaulish hype if you ask me. There's no struggle from behind us at all and they're as light as a feather to pull along!' But when he turns round to check on their captives he finds that they have gone! 'Yes, of course, it's just all Gaulish hype, isn't it?' his partner remarks sarcastically as they wonder how they are going to break the news to their captain. 'Nothing but hype!'

Reduce MAGIC POTION by 1 measure. Go next to 145.

43

'Yes, I'm Spongemix,' the waiter whispers. 'How can I help you? Are you two wanting to join our movement? Or are you messengers from one of the Resistance groups hiding in the woods?' Asterix explains that they are neither – and briefly tells him about their mission. 'You mean *you* are Asterix!' the waiter exclaims. 'Of course, you must be because I've heard you're always accompanied by a fat friend. I'd completely forgotten about that when I hid the other Asterix!' The two Gauls both gawk at him in confusion. 'The *other* Asterix?' they exclaim in unison. ***Go to 182.***

'Is it Fingerlix, then?' Asterix asks after the captain tells them that his name *isn't* Klunkklix. 'Or Seniorservix?' The little Gaul's persistence makes the captain grow suspicious, however. 'What's it to you, squirt?' he demands. 'Are you Roman spies? Roman spies aren't welcome on my ship!' And at that he suddenly blows on a whistle to summon all his crew. 'Take these Romans below deck, men,' he orders fiercely, 'and put them in irons for the rest of the voyage!' **Go to 122.**

The Gauls are just about to bite into their boar-burgers (Asterix's a 'regular', Obelix's a 'quarter-tonner') when a Roman on the next stool notices the gourd at Asterix's belt. He'd been ordered to look out for a puny little Gaul with a gourd! 'That's magic potion in there, isn't it?' he barks at them as he draws out his sword. 'You two are Asterix and Obelix, aren't you? Unless you can tell me the region's password, you're under arrest! Is it bottleneck, blackspot or hold-up?'

If you have picked up the PASSWORD SCROLL during the

adventure, you may use it here to find out the correct password. Do this by placing the SCROLL exactly over the shape below. If you haven't picked up the SCROLL, you'll have to guess at the password.

If you think it's BOTTLENECK	**go to 68**
If you think it's BLACKSPOT	**go to 107**
If you think it's HOLD-UP	**go to 278**

46

'Do you remember that time when we encountered those patrols in the forest near our village and knocked out two hundred Romans in one go?' Asterix reminisces with a chuckle as he and Obelix enter

The Cheese and Onion. 'I heard that most of them didn't come round for several days!' Obelix also has a happy memory. 'And do you remember that time we knocked out *five* hundred Romans?' he asks. 'Some of them didn't come round for several weeks!' Suddenly, though, they both gasp – the inn is full of soldiers! But the soldiers are all intent on minding their own business, nervously drinking or playing dominoes. Having overheard some of the Gauls' conversation, they'd quickly changed their minds about the planned trap, pretending that they hadn't noticed the Gauls! *Go to 149*.

47
THE GAULS
ARE CONFRONTED BY

ROMAN PATROLS HERE

Keep throwing the dice until the Gauls have knocked out this number of patrols. Any magic potions rolled before this total is reached must be deducted from the score on the MAGIC POTION COUNTER. When the Gauls have finished the fight, go to 282.

48

Asterix and Obelix now search the harbour for a ship that will be sailing to *their* part of Gaul. They're in luck. There's one that will be calling at a port only a short distance south of their village. And it's leaving in the next few minutes! *Go to 217*.

49

'Nineteen gold coins for a few bar snacks!' Asterix exclaims to the tavern keeper when he has settled the bill. 'That's outrageous!' The tavern keeper apologises for the high price, gloomily explaining that it's because of all the Roman taxes that have to be added to the bill. 'There's a 30 per cent salt tax for your nuts,' he moans, 'a 50 per cent oil tax for your olives and a 70 per cent breadcrumb tax for the stuffing in your wild boar. And, if that's not enough, they then slap a 17.5 per cent VAT (**V**ictorious **A**rmy **T**ax) on the total!' *Go to 145*.

50

'No wonder the postal delivery is always so slow with those roadblocks holding it up,' Asterix says after they have knocked out all the soldiers. 'Still,' he adds with a wink, 'I suspect it will be a lot quicker now!' As the post-cart finally enters Lugdunum, the tied-up driver in the back attempts to alert the sentries at the gate. But Dogmatix keeps the Roman quiet by snapping at his ankles. 'We post people are always having this sort of problem with dogs!' he grumbles to himself. *Go to 218*.

51
THE GAULS
ARE CONFRONTED BY

ROMAN PATROLS HERE

Keep throwing the dice until the Gauls have knocked out this number of patrols. Any magic potions rolled before this total is reached must be deducted from the score on the MAGIC POTION COUNTER. When the Gauls have finished the fight, go to 180.

52

'And where do you think *you're* going?' Asterix asks the petrified farmer when the Romans are strewn all over his hut. The wretch who had betrayed them for a few gold coins was in fact trying to make his getaway. He was quickly packing those few possessions that hadn't been smashed into a trunk. 'Oh, I just thought that now was the right time to take a holiday,' he answers, all in a sweat. 'You're welcome to stay here during my absence, though. It'll be nice to know that someone's keeping the place warm for me. Well, as warm as can be expected with only half a door left . . . and that gaping hole in the roof, of course.' *Go to 129*.

53

'Want some of my luverly fish stew, ducks?' the plump dark-haired woman asks as the Gauls approach her stall. 'It's the tastiest in Massilia. There's cockles in it and clams and winkles and whelks and . . .' Obelix licks his lips as he hears all this but he's worried about how tiny all the ingredients are. 'Any boar in it?' he asks. The woman shakes her head. 'But there are prawns,' she continues, ' . . . and crayfish . . . and crabs . . . and . . .' Asterix quickly interrupts her, though, asking if they could just have a pot full of the stew to take away. They'll be here all day otherwise! 'That will be three gold coins,' the woman says after she has securely tied the lid on the pot.

If you have picked up the COINBAG during the adventure, you can use this to pay the woman. Rotate the disc to 'count out' the 3 gold coins – then go to the number that appears on the other side of the card. If you don't have the COINBAG, go to 197 instead.

54

'Are you sailing for Lutetia?' Asterix asks the captain as the trio board the boat with the orange sail. The little Gaul's eyes are still warily searching all about him – particularly around the many large wine barrels on deck. There's probably just room in each one for a Roman! His fears are soon allayed, though. The captain tells them that he *is* going to Lutetia – to sell his wine. 'Would you like to try some?' he asks, puncturing one of the barrels with his dagger. A golden-coloured liquid starts to spurt out. There really is just wine in there. And not the *whine* of a punctured Roman either! *Go to 102*.

55
THE GAULS
ARE CONFRONTED BY

ROMAN PATROLS HERE

Keep throwing the dice until the Gauls have knocked out this

number of patrols. Any magic potions rolled before this total is reached must be deducted from the score on the MAGIC POTION COUNTER. When the Gauls have finished the fight, go to 4.

56

'Hey, you can't treat my regulars like that!' the innkeeper complains to Asterix and Obelix as he scurries from one unconscious soldier to another, anxiously trying to bring them round. 'I can't say I like the Romans much but I need their custom!' Asterix puts a reassuring arm round the innkeeper. 'But just consider,' he confides to him with a wink, 'all of those soldiers are probably going to need a stiff double – maybe even a treble – to put them on their feet again. It will be the best day's takings you've ever had!' Seeing the greedy smile grow on the innkeeper's face, Asterix adds, 'So since we've done you a favour, you can do us one. Tell us which boat on the river can be trusted to give us a safe passage to Lutetia!' *Go to 102.*

57

'That worked out at two gold coins per cornet!' Asterix complains once the vendor and his cart have moved on. 'It's terrible how these local people cheat us tourists,' he adds. 'He must have seen you as a real sucker!' Obelix has a think about this for a moment while he consumes his iced goats' milk. 'Well, he got me very wrong, I'm afraid,' he replies indignantly. 'I would say I'm much more of a licker. The only time I do any sucking is right at the end just to get that last little bit out of the cornet!' ***Go to 241***.

'What an exhibition!' Asterix remarks as they follow the veiled belly-dancer from one street to another. 'He's a disgrace to the Roman army!' As they start to move a little closer to him, however, Asterix begins to wonder whether it might be a *real* belly-dancer they're following. Perhaps she is to perform at one of the weekend orgies and she'd gone into the novelty shop just to buy a secret water squirter for when her Roman audience become a little too fresh! He suddenly has an idea how he can find out for sure. He'll run past and snatch off the veil! The idea works . . . but not with the result Asterix had been hoping for. The piercing scream that rents the air most definitely confirms that it *is* a genuine belly-dancer! ***Go to 24***.

'Well, we certainly don't have to worry about being stopped for speeding!' Asterix comments as their horse trots wearily along the road in the slow lane. 'Look, even those long heavy chariots are overtaking us!' The milestones show that Camaracum is gradually getting nearer and nearer, however, and if all goes well it looks as if the Gauls will reach it just before dark. But all doesn't go well! Their poor horse suddenly drops to its knees, unable to go a step further! *Go to 163.*

60
THE GAULS
ARE CONFRONTED BY

ROMAN PATROLS HERE

Keep throwing the dice until the Gauls have knocked out this number of patrols. Any magic potions rolled before this total is reached must be deducted from the score on the MAGIC POTION COUNTER. When the Gauls have finished the fight, go to 268.

61

It's fortunate that Klunkklix *is* the shopkeeper's correct name. Fortunate because at that moment a Roman patrol appears at the door of the shop! 'Quick, hurry through to my stock-room at the back,' Klunkklix whispers to the Gauls. 'There's a secret tunnel there that will take you into the next street. I'll stall them by offering their captain this basket of humbugs. He might not look particularly sweet but I happen to know that he's got a very sweet tooth!' *Go to 257.*

62

Asterix's quick brain suddenly has an idea, however. He insists that the bowls player has a swig of his magic potion, claiming that it will help his concentration. 'Oh look, nasty Romans!' he exclaims as soon as he has got his gourd back again – and then he and Obelix are off! Although the Gauls are in a hurry, they still have time for just a quick look back over their shoulders. The bowls player is hurling one wooden ball after another at the soldiers – and they're whizzing like cannonballs! 'Those poor Romans are going down like ninepins,' Asterix chuckles. 'Literally!'

Reduce MAGIC POTION by 1 measure. Go next to 145.

'Ah, this is a bit more comfortable!' Asterix remarks as he picks up the reins at the front of the post-cart. The Gauls should have remained hidden in the back of the cart for a little longer, though, because they suddenly spot a roadblock ahead of them. Asterix quickly turns the horses towards a detour road on the left but to his horror he sees that there is a contingent of Romans there as well. And also another one blocking the detour road to the right! He seems to have no option but to *charge* one of the roadblocks. It's just a matter of hoping that they choose the weakest one!

Which road do you want them to take?

If detour to left	**go to 55**
If detour to right	**go to 104**
If remain on main road	**go to 148**

64
THE GAULS
ARE CONFRONTED BY

ROMAN PATROLS HERE

Keep throwing the dice until the Gauls have knocked out this number of patrols. Any magic potions rolled before this total is reached must be deducted from the score on the MAGIC POTION COUNTER. When the Gauls have finished the fight, go to 195.

To the relief of Asterix (and the disappointment of Obelix), the captain starts apologising to them. 'Your password is right,' he tells them humbly. 'Please accept my apologies. I shouldn't have doubted you. You obviously do live here. I hope you won't report this unfortunate incident to my superior, though. He does like us to keep good relations with the locals!' Asterix assures him that they won't, and nudges Obelix discreetly towards the door. 'Phew, that was a close one! I think we'd better get out of here as quickly as possible, don't you,' he whispers to his friend. 'Good day to you,' he adds more loudly as he slithers past the captain. Obelix decides to take the courtesies one step further, though. 'Humbug?' he offers him as the captain wishes them good day too. 'Oh no, not again!' Asterix exclaims as he sees the face of the insulted Roman fill with rage . . . and as quickly as he can he yanks Obelix out of the shop and into the street. *Go to 257.*

66
THE GAULS
ARE CONFRONTED BY

ROMAN PATROLS HERE

Keep throwing the dice until the Gauls have knocked out this number of patrols. Any magic potions rolled before this total is reached must be deducted from the score on the MAGIC POTION COUNTER. When the Gauls have finished the fight, go to 252.

'Are you sure your name isn't Chokkybix?' Asterix insists. 'What is it then?' This merely makes the shopkeeper suspicious of him, though, and the Gauls soon find themselves being ushered towards the door. He obviously *is* the Resistance leader. Although Asterix realises it is now too late to gain his trust, he tries to think if there is any way in which he can help him in his struggle against the Romans. Stepping outside the door, he notices the shopkeeper's cat sleeping under the awning–next to a bowl of milk. He discreetly sprinkles a little of his potion into the bowl. It will now be as if a lion were guarding the shop!

Reduce *MAGIC POTION* by 1 measure. Go next to 261.

'Bottleneck is right!' the Roman says a lot more amicably as he puts his sword away again. 'So you two obviously *are* from round here then. I say, talking of bottlenecks, have you ever *seen* the traffic this busy? I'd say it's even worse than last year, wouldn't you?' Asterix pretends to ruminate on this – but Obelix is keen to contribute to the chitchat. 'It's nothing compared to Lutetia, though!' he remarks. 'That's right up in the north of Gaul, only about two days' chariot drive from our little vill–' Asterix quickly yanks Obelix away, though, before he can finish! **Go to 168.**

The Gauls make a thorough search of the crowded inn but the thief is nowhere to be found. When they finally step out of The Cutlass and Parrot, however, they notice a commotion across the street. It's in the doorway of The Skull and Crossbones. A patrol of Romans have just dragged out a man carrying a large shopping bag. *Their* shopping bag! 'They obviously think that that thief is me!' Asterix exclaims as he watches the Romans pour the contents of the bag on to the street and demand an explanation from the man. 'Well, I'm going to have to own up to them that *I'm* me! It's the only way we're going to get the bag back!' *Go to 121.*

70

Asterix realises that his 'code' must have been wrong. The shopkeeper immediately goes white, as if he wishes that he'd been a lot more careful! 'Of course, there isn't really a bag of gold hidden in any of my humbugs,' he says, laughing unconvincingly. 'It's just a selling gimmick. Sometimes I say there's a bag of gold, sometimes that you win a cruise on a luxury galley. Very dishonest of me, I know! Look, why don't you take that pot of humbugs with my compliments and we'll forget all about it.' Normally, Asterix and Obelix might have taken exception to this blatant attempt to humbug them – but they remind themselves that the gold is after all intended for a very worthy cause. So they allow themselves to be brusquely ushered out of the shop without protest! **Go to 257.**

71

Handing Obelix the pot of stew, the woman asks if he would like anything else. 'How about a little saucer of something to eat now . . . mussels?' she asks him. Obelix immediately starts to blush with pride. At last someone who doesn't call him fat! At last someone who realises that that's just *muscle* making up his oversized tummy! But then his pride is completely shattered. 'Or if you don't like mussels, how about scallops?' the woman adds. Asterix can't help chuckling at his friend's misunderstanding. 'Come along, Muscles,' he laughs, dragging him away, ' . . . before you think you're being called *shrimp*!' **Go to 236.**

72

'It would all be so easy, that's what our captain told us!' one of the dazed Romans grumbles as the Gauls calmly disappear round a corner. 'It would be just like three blind mice walking into an alley full of cats, that's what he said. I ask you – did they *look* like blind mice? Do *we* look like cats? Tell me how many cats you know that lie in a great big heap like this.' But his whingeing was falling on deaf ears. And ringing ears! . . . and boxed ears! . . . and cauliflower ears! . . . ***Go to 218***.

IT WOULD ALL BE SO EASY, THAT'S WHAT OUR CAPTAIN TOLD US!

73

'Ah yes, my memory's becoming a little clearer now!' the sailor says after Asterix has begrudgingly paid him his bribe. 'It was The Skull and Crossbones that the person entered! For a few more gold coins I could probably give you a detailed description of what he–' But the Gauls are already out the door and hurrying across the street. And a few minutes later they are reclaiming their shopping bag. 'Oh, that bag that I found belongs to you two, does it?' the thief splutters unconvincingly as the Gauls lift him from the floor. 'How lucky that we bumped into each other. I thought I was going to have to make the long walk to the lost property office!' ***Go to 48***.

The two horses are pulling hard and the Gauls do indeed travel very quickly. But about half-way along their journey to their next destination, they find that they have to cross a wide, fast-flowing river. The river is spanned by four bridges which are all quite close together but of different widths and construction styles. There is *one* thing that they all have in common, though – a sturdy stone guard tower in the middle! So it's just a matter of hoping that the Gauls happen to choose the bridge with the *smallest* number of guards on it . . .

Which bridge do you want them to choose?

If wide stone bridge	**go to 280**
If narrow stone bridge	**go to 116**
If wide wooden bridge	**go to 224**
If narrow wooden bridge	**go to 39**

75
THE GAULS
ARE CONFRONTED BY

ROMAN PATROLS HERE

Keep throwing the dice until the Gauls have knocked out this number of patrols. Any magic potions rolled before this total is reached must be deducted from the score on the MAGIC POTION COUNTER. When the Gauls have finished the fight, go to 143.

76

'Yes, Sandkix *is* my name. How did you know that?' the waiter asks in a whisper as he leans right across the Gauls' table. Asterix explains who they are – and about their wager with the Romans. 'Then you must reach Nicae as quickly as possible!' the waiter responds. 'But what about all these traffic jams?' he adds anxiously. 'Ah, I know how I can help you there. I'll make everyone who comes in here wait three times as long for their food from now on. That should empty the road for you!' *Go to 168*.

77

'Now do be very careful with those corks,' the assistant shouts after the Gauls as they leave the wine shop with the green awning. 'They can be lethal if the bottle is fizzed up too much!' Unfortunately, this is overheard by a passing Roman. 'So you needed to be warned about our explosive wine, did you?' he confronts them, raising his spear. 'That proves that you can't be locals. You're the two *out*laws we're looking *out* for, aren't you?' *Go to 193*.

78

'Now don't forget that he said we must be very careful with this sort of wine,' Asterix warns Obelix as they leave the wine shop. 'Too much shaking about and the bottles could explode in your bag. So that means no bashing Romans and no chasing boar!' Obelix heaves with a huge sob on hearing this – so huge in fact that Asterix is worried that the wine might explode anyway! 'All right, all right!' Asterix tries to calm him. 'I'll allow the Roman-bashing and the boar-chasing on the condition that you always put the bag to one side first. And the same goes for any jumps for joy,' he hurriedly adds on seeing Obelix's delighted reaction. 'You must always put the bag DOWN first!' *Go to 261*.

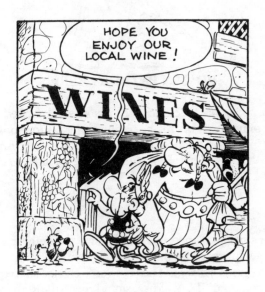

79

'Shall we chuck them all overboard now, into the water?' Obelix asks eagerly when they have knocked out all the Romans on the galley. 'I love hearing that nice splash that they make!' Asterix tells him that there isn't time, though. They must quickly return to their rowing-boat before the other four galleys raise anchor and come after them! 'Hi, Seasix, we're back!' Obelix says when the Gauls have scrambled back down the side of the galley. 'Thanks for minding the rowing-boat for us!' The poor holidaymaker is quite speechless. He was expecting never to see the two Gauls again. And hoping it too! *Go to 40*.

80

THE GAULS
ARE CONFRONTED BY

ROMAN PATROLS HERE

Keep throwing the dice until the Gauls have knocked out this number of patrols. Any magic potions rolled before this total is reached must be deducted from the score on the MAGIC POTION COUNTER. When the Gauls have finished the fight, go to 144.

81

'Oh, that's right – flamenco was the previous month's password,' Asterix says quickly after the Roman has told him that it is wrong. 'This month's is *mañana*. The passwords change so frequently I often get confused!' To Asterix's astonishment, the Roman looks as if he might be taken in by this piece of desperation. But to his even greater astonishment, Obelix then goes and ruins it all for them. 'Yes, this month's password is definitely *mañana*,' he smiles innocently at the Roman. He then turns towards Asterix. 'By the way, Asterix,' he asks, 'what does this funny word *mañana* mean?' *Go to 256.*

'Look what your fun and games have cost us!' Obelix tells his dog crossly as they leave the fish stall. 'NINE gold coins!' Instead of feeling remorse, though, Dogmatix just starts to sulk. *Oh yes, it's all right for those two to go scrapping with the Romans, isn't it?* he thinks to himself moodily. *All the broken tables and things don't matter then. But as soon as I cause a little mess, I'm in the dog-house!* Dogmatix gives another moody sniff, dragging his tail along the ground. It really is a dog's life! *Go to 211.*

Asterix has *nothing* to say for himself just at the moment. All his efforts are devoted to standing on Obelix's foot. He's desperately trying to stop his friend walking over and thumping the centurion for calling him fat! 'Yes, there's something suspicious about you, little man!' the centurion continues, pointing a menacing finger at Asterix. 'If you're a *true* sailor, you should know the correct password for these waters. Is it hearties, swabbie or seadog?

If you have picked up the PASSWORD SCROLL during the adventure, you may consult it here to find out the correct password. You do this by placing the SCROLL exactly over the shape below. If you haven't picked up the SCROLL, you'll have to guess the password.

If you think it's HEARTIES   **go to 154**
If you think it's SWABBIE   **go to 249**
If you think it's SEADOG   **go to 287**

84

The man wipes the perspiration from his brow in great relief. 'So I *can* trust you!' he exclaims. 'You *do* know my name! Was it Hayrix who told you about me, a cattle farmer way up north?' Asterix confirms that it was – and then explains the nature of his mission.

'Well yes, of course I can direct you to a butcher,' the man says to them enthusiastically when Asterix has at last finished telling the man his tale. 'I won't send you to Gastrix's shop just in the next street because his meat often looks a bit green. You must go to a wonderful little place in *rue Theday* where it's always very fresh and tasty. I'm sure you wouldn't want to serve your Roman guest anything but the very best, would you?' he says, sharing a little chuckle with them. ***Go to 96.***

85

'Are we *still* stowaways?' Obelix asks innocently after Asterix has reluctantly paid the captain the sixteen gold coins. Asterix angrily puts his hands on his hips. 'Oh, it's nice to know you've got the word right at last!' he exclaims. 'Well, no, we're *not* stowaways now. We're bona fide paying passengers!' Obelix starts to sulk at Asterix's tone but then he suddenly brightens again. 'Do bona fide paying passengers hide under lifeboats as well?' he asks eagerly. ***Go to 217.***

The Gauls now search the harbour for a ship that will be sailing to *their* part of Gaul. They in fact find *three*: all scheduled to stop off at a port which is only a very short distance south of their village. One is due to set sail in ten minutes, one in twenty minutes and one in half an hour. 'The most obvious ship to choose is the one leaving first,' Asterix says as he thoughtfully strokes his chin. 'But that doesn't necessarily mean it will *arrive* first. It might not be quite as fast as the other two. So I'm afraid it's going to be a bit of pot-luck!'

Which ship will you choose for them?

If ship leaving in ten minutes	**go to 170**
If ship leaving in twenty minutes	**go to 134**
If ship leaving in thirty minutes	**go to 19**

With their shoes dangling from their necks by their tied laces, Asterix and Obelix quickly slip into the water. They swim quietly from one boat to the other – from the one with a ram figurehead at the front . . . to the one with a horse figurehead . . . to the one with a goat figurehead. *Still*, though, they can't be sure whether any of them have Romans hidden secretly on board! 'We'll just have to

hope for the best,' says Asterix, as they now prepare to scramble up the side of one of the boats.

Which of the three boats do you want this to be?

If boat with ram figurehead	**go to 254**
If boat with horse figurehead	**go to 7**
If boat with goat figurehead	**go to 196**

88

'I shouldn't have let my suspicions about that signpost drop!' Asterix says, cross with himself, as they now walk out the other side of the devastated Roman camp. 'It obviously *had* been twisted round after all!' Obelix looks rather less annoyed with himself, however. In fact, he could best be described as looking quite pleased! 'Yes, but just think, Asterix,' he tells his friend, 'if you *hadn't* trusted the signpost, then you would have decided to follow one of the arms that pointed to a Roman camp. Can't you see what the awful outcome would have been? There might not have really been a Roman camp there at all!' ***Go to 263***.

89

When the captain tells him that his password was wrong, Asterix becomes indignant. 'Well, how am I meant to know what the password is?' he asks irritably. 'The whole *point* of being an outlaw is that we don't recognise the Roman passwords!' The captain concedes that he has something there. 'All right, I agree that you are more likely to be the wanted outlaws than this man here,' he says, boxing the thief's ears. 'So you'd better take this shopping bag. It seems that it's rightly yours!' It's only some time after our heroes have left the scene that the captain suddenly realises that, if the bag *was* theirs, he should have arrested them! ***Go to 48***.

90

'What's on your tray, love?' the lady at the end of the counter asks Obelix as the Gauls queue up to pay for their food. 'Let me have a look. Three whole boar, roasted . . . three whole boar, baked . . . three whole boar, boiled . . . and a couple of boar sausages. They'll be for your little dog, will they? Nice little thing, isn't he? That will be eighteen gold coins please!'

If you have picked up the COINBAG during the adventure, you can use this to pay the lady. Rotate the disc to 'count out' the 18 gold coins – then go to the number that appears on the other side of the card. If you don't have the COINBAG, go to 284 instead.

91

Since the man in the boat doesn't respond to Nosepix, Asterix tries Spongemix. But the man doesn't look up when he calls out that name either. He's just about to try Chokkybix when he suddenly feels something dripping on his feet. It's his magic potion – the gourd has a small puncture! 'We're going to have to get to a shop as quickly as possible and buy a new one,' he tells Obelix desperately. 'Otherwise our cause is lost!' They eventually manage to find a gourd shop but when Asterix carefully transfers his potion to the new receptacle he discovers that he's a whole measure short.

Reduce MAGIC POTION by 1 measure. Go next to 174.

92
THE GAULS
ARE CONFRONTED BY

ROMAN PATROLS HERE

Keep throwing the dice until the Gauls have knocked out this

number of patrols. Any magic potions rolled before this total is reached must be deducted from the score on the MAGIC POTION COUNTER. When the Gauls have finished the fight, go to 21.

93

'Green is wrong!' the farmer retorts. 'So you're *not* Asterix after all! I knew you were far too puny!' Obelix scratches his head in confusion. 'So does that mean you're not going to do those nice drawings for us after all?' he asks innocently. The farmer laughs in his face. 'Of course it means I'm not going to do those nice drawings for you, you fat dunce!' he says. Obelix immediately sees red . . . but so do several bulls, unfortunately, in a neighbouring field. As Obelix makes a grab at him, the farmer quickly unties his red neckerchief and waves it in the direction of the bulls. They immediately respond to his sign for help and start to charge our heroes. 'I think we'd better just forget about those sketches, don't you?' Asterix pants as they leap over a fence just in time. *Go to 227.*

94

'Let them through, men!' the captain orders his soldiers. 'Their password is correct. It looks like they are local fisherman after all!' The Gauls hold their breath as they step towards the gap opened up for them. They can't believe the Romans fell for it! But as they are squeezing through the gap, one of the Romans remarks that there is something fishy about them. Or, rather, there *isn't* anything fishy about them. They don't smell of fish at all! ***Go to 179***.

95

Stealthily making their way down to the left of the bridge, the Gauls creep along the bank, keeping themselves hidden behind some bushes. 'What can you see?' Asterix whispers. 'Some bushes!' Obelix replies. His little friend has to bite his tongue to stop himself losing patience. 'No, I mean what can you see if you peep *through* the bushes? There are three large boats moored there. Can you see any sign that there might be Romans hiding on board any of them?' Obelix shakes his head – but Asterix is still rather doubtful about the boats. He can't hesitate all day, though. The captain of each boat looks as if he's about to set sail at any moment and so the Gauls are going to have to hurry up one of the gangplanks fast.

Which boat will you make them board?

If boat with red sail	**go to 15**
If boat with white sail	**go to 120**
If boat with orange sail	**go to 54**

96

Asterix and Obelix finally spot a nice-looking butcher's and they cross the street towards it. They leave Dogmatix at the door while they step inside to purchase their ham. They find themselves having to wait behind a bumptious Roman, though, who is ordering titbits for his commander's orgy on Saturday night. 'And I'll have three hundred boar's ears on cocktail sticks,' he demands of the flustered butcher. 'Make sure they're the best you have because they're for the *Governor* of Lutetia. He's given me his password scroll should you need proof. As you know, only very important persons are granted these. The passwords written here allow freedom of movement right through Gaul!' Hearing this, Asterix eagerly peers over the Roman's shoulder, trying to catch a glimpse of the scroll . . . *Go to 136.*

97

**THE GAULS
ARE CONFRONTED BY**

ROMAN PATROLS HERE

Keep throwing the dice until the Gauls have knocked out this number of patrols. Any magic potions rolled before this total is reached must be deducted from the score on the MAGIC POTION COUNTER. When the Gauls have finished the fight, go to 183.

98

'Your answer is *wrong*!' the farmer replies. 'It looks as if I was right about you being Roman spies then!' he adds triumphantly. But his cocky grin starts to fade as it slowly dawns on him what this actually means! 'Of course, I'm not *really* the leader of the local Resistance,' he stammers with a poor attempt at a chuckle. 'That was just me trying to make myself sound important. No, I'm merely a simple farmer. All I do is milk these stupid cows all day. The job's so boring that sometimes I have little resistance to it. Yes, that's what I meant about resistance – resistance to milking cows all . . . ' But Asterix and Obelix have had enough. It's clear that they are going to obtain no more assistance from the farmer and so they continue on their way. *Go to 227*.

99

The cart-driver stayed outside the inn during the punch-up. When he sees not eighty Romans emerge but just Asterix and Obelix, his jaw nearly falls to the ground! Asterix begins to grow suspicious about him. 'If it wasn't for the fact that he's useful to take us the rest of the way to Durocortorum,' he whispers to his friend, 'I'd probably give him a good thumping as well. I'm sure there's something fishy about him but I just can't prove it.' Obelix gives a proud smile. 'Oh, I can,' he says simply. 'I've known it ever since we first set eyes on him. That wine barrel of his is as light as a feather. It's completely empty!' Asterix quite despairs when he hears his friend say this. 'Now he tells me!' he says to himself. Asterix can't help thinking that the wine barrel is not the only thing that's completely empty! *Go to 137*.

'Champagne is wrong!' the Roman barks at them, raising his spear again. 'As if we would invent a silly word like that!' Asterix wonders how they're going to escape – but then he remembers about those lethal corks. He quickly shakes one of the wine bottles, aiming it at the Roman. The exploding cork hits him right on the jaw! 'I don't think it's just *sham pain*!' Asterix chuckles as the Roman rolls about, groaning, on the ground. But the last laugh is on Asterix himself. For he too was thrown to the ground by the force of the explosion. As a result, another cork came out – the cork to his magic potion gourd! Some of the potion leaks away before he has time to force the cork back in again.

Reduce your MAGIC POTION by 1 measure. Go next to 261.

Our heroes finally reach Camaracum and, as they relax on their straw beds after a hearty supper, Obelix asks what food the town is famous for. 'It's not wild boar pie, by any chance?' he asks hopefully. 'Or perhaps wild boar pâté?' Asterix shakes his head at him. 'Humbugs!' he replies. Obelix quite understandably takes exception to this. 'Well, there's no need to be so rude about it,' he snaps. 'How am *I* meant to know what the speciality is here?' Asterix starts to chuckle at his friend's indignation. 'No, when I said "humbugs", I meant *humbugs*,' he explains. 'Those little boiled sweets tasting of peppermint. *They* are what Camaracum is famous for. So the first thing we do tomorrow is look for a sweet shop!' *Go to 156*.

102

Having had a good night's sleep on the boat, the Gauls sail gently into Lutetia early the next morning. 'It looks like rush hour is starting!' Asterix remarks anxiously as they begin to explore the capital. The streets are rapidly growing busier and busier, ox-drawn carts everywhere! 'Let's try and purchase our proof that we've been here as quickly as possible so we can escape this mayhem,' he suggests. 'I believe ham is the food Lutetia is most famous for. We must find a butcher's shop!' As they are searching for a butcher, though, Asterix suddenly yanks Obelix's sleeve! *Go to 177*.

103

'Oh look – hic – it's the Romans we're meant to fight,' a sozzled soldier nudges his snoring friend as Asterix leads the way into The Running Boar. 'Hic – I mean Gauls. We're Romans, aren't we? Or are we the Gauls?' The horrified cart-driver suddenly yanks the Gauls outside again. The drunken soldier is starting to wave to him! 'I-I-I d-don't know what the p-place is coming to,' the cart-driver stammers, breaking into a sweat. 'I'll never dr-drink here again. I'll just give my horse a few seconds at the water trough and then I think we'd better be on our way!' *Go to 137*.

104
THE GAULS
ARE CONFRONTED BY

ROMAN PATROLS HERE

Keep throwing the dice until the Gauls have knocked out this number of patrols. Any magic potions rolled before this total is reached must be deducted from the score on the MAGIC POTION COUNTER. When the Gauls have finished the fight, go to 50.

105
'It's one of those stupid wooden balls!' Asterix exclaims furiously as he discovers what made him trip. 'There ought to be a law against playing ball games in the street!' He is soon on his feet again, though, and he and Obelix eventually lose the pursuing Romans. But then Asterix happens to glance down at his belt. To his horror, he sees that the cork is missing from his gourd of magic potion. It must have come out when he tripped! It's no problem to replace the cork with another one, of course . . . but what can't be replaced is

any magic potion that was spilt. And it looks as if it was a whole measure!

Reduce MAGIC POTION by 1 measure. Go next to 145.

106
'Then I did make a mistake about you,' the shopkeeper says with a shake of his head. 'You're *not* the go-betweens who have come to collect the bag of gold coins. If you had been, you would have asked for the *box* of humbugs, not the basket.' He feels so embarrassed by his mistake that he tells the Gauls that they can have their basket of humbugs free, with his compliments. 'It's the least I can give you,' he says, 'after making you think that you would be walking out of my shop with a bag full of gold!' **Go to 257.**

107
The Roman tells them that their password is wrong and that he's going to take them in. 'Hands on heads and walk slowly towards my chariot outside!' he orders. Asterix enquires if the journey to their

prison is likely to be long. Since the answer is yes, he asks if he might first spend a quick denarius (we would say 'spend a quick penny'). As soon as he is inside 'the warriors' (we would say 'the gents'), though, Asterix downs a measure of his magic potion. He then bursts back out again. 'Obelix!' he tuts furiously on finding the Roman laid out on the floor. 'Didn't you see me wink at you? I've now drunk some of my magic potion for nothing!'

Reduce MAGIC POTION by 1 measure. Go next to 168.

108

'You check the tables to our right and I'll check those to our left,' Asterix tells his friend as they step into the grimy and rowdy interior of The Skull and Crossbones. Asterix carefully scrutinises every customer on his side but Obelix is soon distracted by a delicious

smell wafting through the inn. It's roast boar! Asterix is just about to tell him off for this lack of concentration when his gaze falls on one of the waiters. He exactly fits the farmer's description of the Burdigala Resistance leader! Asterix tries to remember his name so he can discreetly approach him. Was it Seniorservix, Klunkklix or Spongemix?

If you have picked up the SKETCHPAD during the adventure, you may consult it here to find out the man's name. If not, you'll have to guess which of the three possibilities Asterix should give.

If you prefer SENIORSERVIX   **go to 201**
If you prefer KLUNKKLIX   **go to 125**
If you prefer SPONGEMIX   **go to 43**

109

'This horse doesn't exactly live life in the fast lane, does it?' Asterix comments as it trots wearily along in the slow lane of the road. Nevertheless, the milestones show Camaracum gradually getting nearer and nearer and it looks as if they might just reach the town before nightfall. Suddenly, though, they come upon a banner across the road which warns of two roadblocks ahead, one in each lane. It orders all chariots to stop there for inspection! *Go to 231.*

110

'Twenty gold coins!' Asterix exclaims. 'Hand those cornets straight back to him, Obelix! We don't have that sort of money – and even if we did, I strongly object to paying these extortionate tourist prices!' The vendor indignantly insists that his prices aren't extortionate, though. He explains that the ice has to be collected from high up in the mountains and then brought down very quickly before it melts. He says it's very tiring and stressful work. 'All right, all right . . . ' Asterix yields eventually. 'We can't pay you any gold coins, but I'll let you have a little of my magic potion as payment instead. You'll then be able to race up and down the mountains in a fraction of the time!'

Reduce MAGIC POTION by 1 measure. Go next to 241.

111

'What do you mean, that pot of stew has a long way to travel?' the Roman enquires of Asterix. 'Is that because you come right from the other end of Gaul?' he demands keenly, seeing the prospect of instant promotion. Asterix pretends to be amused by this idea, though. 'No, we're from Spain,' he laughs nonchalantly. 'We're bullfighters taking a little holiday. When you're being tossed and gored all year round, you need to get away for a few – ' But the unconvinced Roman brusquely interrupts him. 'What's this month's password for Spain, then?' he demands. 'If you're really from there, you should be able to tell me whether it's paella, flamenco or *mañana*.'

If you have picked up the PASSWORD SCROLL during the

adventure, you may consult it here to find out the correct password. You do this by placing the SCROLL exactly over the shape below. If you haven't picked up the SCROLL, you'll have to guess the password.

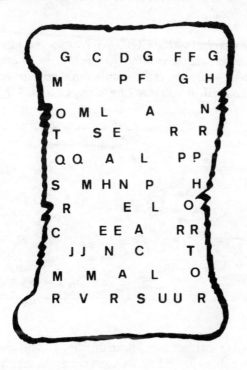

If you think it's PAELLA   **go to 131**
If you think it's FLAMENCO   **go to 81**
If you think it's MAÑANA   **go to 222**

112

The Gauls have just purchased a large pot of stew from the plump red-haired woman when Dogmatix suddenly darts underneath her stall. He has spotted a cat there – and cats to Dogmatix are like Romans to his master! There's nothing he likes better than having a good scrap with them! But by the time Dogmatix has finished the scrap, the stall is a complete mess. There's not one bucket of fish that hasn't been knocked over! 'Look what your horrible dog has done to all my beautiful fish!' the woman cries furiously. 'I can't possibly sell them now. You must give me nine gold coins as compensation!'

If you have picked up the COINBAG during the adventure, use this to compensate the woman. Rotate the disc to 'count out' the 9 gold coins – then go to the number that appears on the other side of the card. If you don't have the COINBAG, go to 240.

113
. . . straight for a blockade of Roman galleys! The five warships are waiting for them just round the next corner of the coast. 'Oops!' Asterix exclaims as he finally spots them and realises that it is too late now to do anything but try and break through part of the line. He wonders which galley they should steer towards . . .

Which will you decide for them?

If galley nearest coast	**go to 172**
If galley second nearest coast	**go to 221**
If galley in middle	**go to 64**
If galley second furthest from coast	**go to 75**
If galley furthest from coast	**go to 142**

I'LL KNOCK!
BUT BE CAREFUL THIS TIME!

114

'Thank goodness you chose this hut and not one of the other two in the valley!' the farmer exclaims as he yanks the trio inside and quickly slams the door behind them. 'The Romans have bribed their owners to let them hide there. I never did like my two neighbours much! Come, I'll show you to the room I've prepared for you.' Exhausted from all the walking they have done that day, Asterix immediately collapses on to the cosy straw bed. But Obelix can't wait for their supper to be brought up and hungrily paces the room. He's sure from the smell wafting up from below that it's wild boar. And perhaps he can just sniff a little sprig of parsley with it as well! ***Go to 129***.

115

'Don't you worry, just leave those Romans to us,' Nosepix reassures Asterix quickly. 'I'll simply tell them that our game of bowls is at a very crucial stage and if they dare to charge through the middle of the balls and disturb them, there are likely to be riots throughout Massilia. The Romans know full well how seriously bowls is taken here!' So the Gauls hurriedly bid Nosepix goodbye and make their escape. 'Can you believe that calmness?' Asterix exclaims with admiration as he and Obelix disappear round a corner. 'His enemies are fast approaching and he just nonchalantly continues with his game of bowls! Surely only a Gaul would show that nerve? You couldn't imagine it of a Briton, for instance, could you!' ***Go to 145***.

116
THE GAULS
ARE CONFRONTED BY

ROMAN PATROLS HERE

Keep throwing the dice until the Gauls have knocked out this number of patrols. Any magic potions rolled before this total is reached must be deducted from the score on the MAGIC POTION COUNTER. When the Gauls have finished the fight, go to 216.

117

'No, Chokkybix is *not* my name!' the man tells them abruptly when Asterix and Obelix have approached him and enquired politely. 'Now buzz off. This is a vital ball I'm about to roll and you're completely ruining my concentration!' It's just then that Asterix spots a patrol of Romans hurrying along the quay towards them. 'They must have spotted us!' he whispers anxiously to Obelix. 'What can we do? We must continue on our journey. We don't have the time to spare for a punch-up now!' ***Go to 62***.

As the Gauls are walking towards the south end of the beach, Asterix suddenly stops dead in his tracks. 'Look at that man down there!' he exclaims, pointing towards the sand. 'The one that's just had a swim and is drying his hair. He fits the description of the

Resistance leader in this town exactly!' They both desperately try to think of the name of the Resistance leader here so that they can introduce themselves and see what assistance he might be able to give them. They remember that his name's definitely either Sandkix, Fingerlix or Nosepix.

If you have picked up the SKETCHPAD during the adventure, you may consult it here to find out the man's name. If not, you'll have to guess which of the three possibilities Asterix should give.

If you prefer SANDKIX	**go to 272**
If you prefer FINGERLIX	**go to 141**
If you prefer NOSEPIX	**go to 34**

'We're never going to finish our tour at this rate,' Asterix exclaims as he washes one item after another, passing them to Obelix to dry. 'These stacks of dirty platters don't seem any lower than when we started. I think it's a case for desperate measures. A *measure* of my magic potion to be precise!' So Asterix immediately uncorks his gourd of magic potion and takes a good swig. When the tavern keeper strolls into the kitchen a few seconds later, he simply can't believe his eyes. Asterix and Obelix have disappeared . . . but so too has all the washing-up. All that's left is just row upon row of gleaming platters!

Reduce MAGIC POTION by 1 measure. Go next to 145.

120
THE GAULS
ARE CONFRONTED BY

ROMAN PATROLS HERE

Keep throwing the dice until the Gauls have knocked out this number of patrols. Any magic potions rolled before this total is reached must be deducted from the score on the MAGIC POTION COUNTER. When the Gauls have finished the fight, go to 228.

121

'Excuse me, Romans,' Asterix addresses them cheekily as he strolls up to the group in the street, 'but I'm afraid there's been a slight case of mistaken identity here. I think you'll find that *I* am Asterix!' The Romans all scoff at this, assuming the little squirt to be crazy. But then one of them becomes intrigued by Obelix. 'Perhaps this person *is* Asterix after all,' he says. Then he has a private word with his captain. 'Do you remember being told that he was travelling with a companion who had a weight problem . . . and looked a bit simple?' ***Go to 226***.

122

'Both prisoners securely in irons, cap'n!' one of the crew reports a few minutes later. 'Shall we give them five hundred lashes as well?' The captain tells him that the irons will be enough, though. To be honest, he's beginning to wonder whether they are Roman spies after all! Maybe that little one was *Asterix* – the valiant Roman-fighter whom he'd been ordered to try and help if he came his way. A few seconds later, the captain has confirmation of this. Asterix suddenly reappears on the upper deck, his chains in contemptuous tatters over his shoulder! Mind you, this demonstration of his superhuman strength did cost Asterix a precious measure of his potion . . .

Reduce MAGIC POTION by 1 measure. Go next to 217.

The shopkeeper is just handing the Gauls their basket of black and white humbugs when the door suddenly flies open behind them. There's a fat Roman captain standing there, accompanied by at least a dozen soldiers. 'Hey, you two!' he yells at Asterix and Obelix. 'Do you live in this town – or are you the two travelling Gauls that we're on the lookout for?' Obelix really wants to give them their answer with his fist . . . but Asterix prefers to see if they can wriggle out of the situation first. 'Yes, we do happen to live here,' he replies nonchalantly. 'I'm an innkeeper and my friend here is a humble tailor.' ***Go to 5***.

'How did you know my name?' the shopkeeper asks with a smile that makes his nose glow even redder. 'Where do you come from? Are you two Asterix and Obelix by any chance?' When the Gauls confirm that they are, the shopkeeper immediately hands them another bottle of fizzy wine. 'This one is not for you but for any Romans that might want to search your bag,' he explains as he carefully hands it to them. 'Make sure that they test some of it. Just a few drops will be enough. It has a super strength fizz that will give them such uncontrollable hiccups that they'll be quite helpless against you!' *Go to 261*.

125

Since Klunkklix obviously isn't the waiter's name, Asterix wonders which one he should try next. Seniorservix or Spongemix? 'Perhaps you would like to have a guess this time?' he asks, turning to Obelix. But his overgrown friend isn't there! Looking all round for him, Asterix just catches a glimpse of him disappearing into the kitchen. He obviously couldn't resist that delicious smell of food wafting by a moment longer! 'Obelix! Don't you realise how serious this is?' Asterix yells crossly as he races after him into the kitchen. But he immediately has to forgive his friend . . . for, trying to cower behind some sacks of vegetables in the corner, is the thief! 'Oh, w-would this sh-shopping b-bag be yours?' the wretch stammers as a very angry Asterix ominously approaches him . . . *Go to 48*.

126
THE GAULS
ARE CONFRONTED BY

ROMAN PATROLS HERE

Keep throwing the dice until the Gauls have knocked out this number of patrols. Any magic potions rolled before this total is reached must be deducted from the score on the MAGIC POTION COUNTER. When the Gauls have finished the fight, go to 275.

127

'This was a good suggestion of yours!' Asterix says as he starts on the delicious boar chop before him. 'I'm feeling a lot more relaxed now, thank you.' But Obelix isn't feeling particularly relaxed. In fact, he's growing less and less relaxed by the second. What use was this tiny little morsel on his plate? 'When I ordered boar, I meant a *whole* boar,' he snaps at a passing waiter. Asterix suddenly jumps as the

irritated waiter turns round. He's sure that's one of the Resistance leaders the farmer described! He quickly tries to think of the name they were given. Was it Sandkix, Spongemix or Fingerlix?

If you have picked up the SKETCHPAD during the adventure,

you may consult it here to find out the waiter's name. If not, you'll have to guess which of the three possibilities Asterix should give.

If you prefer SANDKIX	**go to 76**
If you prefer SPONGEMIX	**go to 14**
If you prefer FINGERLIX	**go to 266**

128

'Well, what else can you offer me?' the sailor asks when Asterix tells him he doesn't have eleven gold coins. 'What about that little gourd you have there? I bet it's full of best sailor's rum, isn't it?' Since Asterix is so desperate, he pretends that it is – and quickly pours a measure of the potion into the sailor's goblet. 'Mmm, a little weaker than what I'm used to – but not bad!' the sailor considers before the potion has started to take effect. 'The man you're after disappeared into The Skull and Crossbones, by the way. Hey, wait a minute. This rum really has quite a punch to –' But the Gauls can't wait. They hare across the street and barge into The Skull and Crossbones. A short while later, they are emerging again . . . having recovered their shopping bag from the trembling thief!

Reduce MAGIC POTION by 1 measure. Go next to 48.

Our heroes rise early, leaving the hut just after the cock crows. But it's not until late afternoon that they finally spot the town of Rotomagus. It lies in a quiet wooded valley just below them, on the opposite bank of a wide river. 'Well, there are certainly plenty of large boats down there,' Asterix remarks. 'But can we be sure that there aren't Romans hiding on some of them, waiting for us? I wonder if those boats on the left of the bridge would be safest? Or maybe those on the right? Or perhaps it would be wisest actually to cross the bridge and enter the town? We might be able to find out there which boats we can trust.'

Which of these three options will you choose for them?

If approach left of bridge	**go to 95**
If approach right of bridge	**go to 208**
If cross the bridge	**go to 253**

130

Obelix grins with satisfaction as the last of the Romans goes flying high into the trees, finishing up wrapped round a branch. But then he notices that his little friend looks rather thoughtful and concerned. Hasn't he enjoyed the fight? 'We're not here to enjoy ourselves,' Asterix replies rather sharply. 'You're forgetting that Getafix told us to try and avoid the Romans, not walk straight into their traps. We must be a lot more careful next time.' Obelix agrees with him . . . but he still can't take that satisfied grin off his face. And it soon makes Asterix grin a little too. He decides that Obelix's attitude is right. On those occasions when they *don't* manage to avoid the Romans, they might just as well at least enjoy it! *Go to 25*.

131

'Paella is wrong!' the Roman barks at them, drawing his sword. 'So you're not Spanish at all. Bullfighters indeed! *I'd* make a better bullfighter than you two yokels!' Obelix wants to give the Roman a good drubbing for this insult but Asterix holds him back. He thinks it would be a lot more fun to put the Roman's boast to the test! 'But where do we get a bull from?' Obelix asks bewilderedly. Asterix gives him a little wink for reply . . . *Go to 36*.

132
THE GAULS
ARE CONFRONTED BY

ROMAN PATROLS HERE

Keep throwing the dice until the Gauls have knocked out this number of patrols. Any magic potions rolled before this total is reached must be deducted from the score on the MAGIC POTION COUNTER. When the Gauls have finished the fight, go to 209.

'I wish he knew what he looked like!' Asterix remarks scornfully as they follow the Greek goddess down the street. 'That wig looks quite ridiculous on him and his dress is positively bursting at the seams!' As they discreetly move right behind the Greek goddess, however, they discover that it's not the Roman after all. It really *is* a woman inside that outfit. 'I still say she's far too big for it!' Asterix insists grumpily as they realise that the Roman and his password scroll will be far away by now. *Go to 24.*

'What did you say we are called again, Asterix?' his friend asks as the trio hide underneath the upturned lifeboat on the ship. 'STOWAWAYS!' Asterix has to repeat for the umpteenth time. 'Now will you be QUIET, Obelix,' he adds irritably, 'or someone will hear us and we'll be thrown off!' But as the ship sails out to sea, Obelix can't help getting the giggles. It's rather fun, this stowaway business! 'WILL YOU BE QUI–' Asterix starts to rebuke him again but it's too late. The ship's captain has discovered them! 'Your passage will cost you sixteen gold coins,' he tells them fiercely. 'If you don't pay up, you'll be thrown to the sharks!'

If you have picked up the COINBAG during the adventure, you can use this to pay for the Gauls' passage. Rotate the disc to 'count out' the 16 gold coins – then go to the number that appears on the other side of the card. If you don't have the COINBAG, go to 204 instead.

'No, I'm not Freekix,' the man yells at them. 'It's just as I thought. You're ROMAN SPIES!' The busy street suddenly turns deathly quiet at the words, a hundred pairs of glaring eyes suddenly turning on Asterix and Obelix. 'Ever get the feeling that someone doesn't like you?' Asterix says, gulping behind his hand. 'Come on. I think we'd better make a run for it!' The three friends dash from one street to another, the angry lynch mob never far behind them. They at last manage to lose the mob, however, and flop against an alley wall to recover their breath. 'I'm going to have to take a measure of my magic potion,' Asterix pants. 'I feel as if I've just run the marathon!'

Reduce MAGIC POTION by 1 measure. Go next to 96.

136

Unfortunately, however, the Roman allows the butcher only the briefest of glimpses at the scroll before nervously tucking it under his belt again. It obviously really *is* as valuable as he's boasting! 'We must try to take that from him without him knowing,' Asterix whispers to his friend. 'We'll do it outside in the busy streets. It will be a lot easier to jostle him there!' So as soon as the Roman has finally left the shop, Asterix moves up to the counter himself and hurriedly asks for his joint of ham . . . ***Go to 205.***

137

It's only a couple of hours later that the Gauls are on foot again, strolling through the narrow streets of Durocortorum. Wherever they look, there seem to be wine shops! 'Will they insist on knowing what our special occasion is before they sell us this fizzy wine?' Obelix asks uncertainly. Asterix shrugs his shoulders. 'Well, if they do,' he replies, 'we'll just say it's for a banquet to humiliate the Romans. I'm sure they'll agree that you can't get a more special occasion than that! Now, which of these shops shall we honour with our custom? The one with the green awning, the one with the red awning or the one with the yellow awning?'

Which will you choose for them?

<blockquote>

If shop with green awning   **go to 77**

If shop with red awning   **go to 286**

If shop with yellow awning   **go to 17**
</blockquote>

138
THE GAULS
ARE CONFRONTED BY

ROMAN PATROLS HERE

Keep throwing the dice until the Gauls have knocked out this number of patrols. Any magic potions rolled before this total is reached must be deducted from the score on the MAGIC POTION COUNTER. When the Gauls have finished the fight, go to 274.

139

'Will you STOP TITTERING!' Asterix whispers irritably to his friend as they lie amongst the mail-bags in the back of the first class post-cart. 'That Roman driving the cart is going to realise that there's something afoot. And talking of feet, will you please get that big foot of yours out of my face!' The uncomfortable journey lasts all night . . . and then into the next day. Asterix finally decides that he can't stand it a moment longer and so suggests that they swap places with the driver, tying him up and putting *him* with the mail-bags! *Go to 63.*

140

Since he doesn't have six gold coins, Asterix offers the shopkeeper a measure of his magic potion for the bottles of fizzy wine. 'Mm, an impertinent little thing,' the shopkeeper considers as he samples the potion, holding it up to the light. 'A surprisingly robust body as well. Okay, it's a deal!' As soon as they have left the wine shop, Asterix gives his friend a nudge in the ribs. 'He'll soon be finding out just *how* impertinent it is!' he chuckles. 'And I rather think *he* will be the one with the robust body. Let's just hope some bossy Romans walk into his shop!'

Reduce MAGIC POTION by 1 measure. Go next to 261.

141

'Yes, my name *is* Fingerlix!' the man exclaims as the Gauls approach him. His voice immediately drops to a cautious whisper. 'You're the two northerners, aren't you?' he asks confidentially behind his towel. 'And you have come to me for my expert local knowledge?' He stealthily glances to left and right again before imparting this. 'Well, make sure you tan no more than half an hour on each side to begin with,' he whispers, 'or you'll end up like lobsters. And be wary of those iced goats' milk sellers. They really rip the tourists off!' Asterix is quite speechless. No wonder *this* part of Gaul hasn't been able to hold out against the Romans. Even its Resistance Movement has gone soft! ***Go to 241.***

THE GAULS
ARE CONFRONTED BY

ROMAN PATROLS HERE

Keep throwing the dice until the Gauls have knocked out this number of patrols. Any magic potions rolled before this total is reached must be deducted from the score on the MAGIC POTION COUNTER. When the Gauls have finished the fight, go to 161.

143

'You mean that was *you two* doing all the thumping I could hear up there?' the holidaymaker asks in disbelief as Asterix and Obelix scramble back down from the galley and return to the rowing-boat. Obelix shows even greater disbelief, though. 'Well, you didn't think it was the Romans, did you?' he asks bewilderedly. 'How *could* it have been? There were only five patrols of them on board. That's barely fifty soldiers!' Trying to make sense of this, the poor holidaymaker starts to wonder who's had the most sun. This weird overgrown stranger . . . or himself! *Go to 40.*

144

'Of course, I never really *wanted* to join the army,' one of the concussed Romans moans to his friend as the Gauls resume their pleasant mountain stroll, disappearing into the distance. 'Well, I did,' he adds, rubbing the growing lump on the top of his head, 'but

I didn't think it would be like this. I thought it would all be exotic travel and pillage. That's what the Legionary Careers place told me. This centurion there said that there would be as much pillage as I wanted. And a smart uniform. Well, I suppose the uniform is quite smart but I really don't think much of . . . ' He suddenly realises that he is wasting his breath, though. His friend is completely out! *Go to 40*.

145

'We must complete the final part of our journey as quickly as possible,' Asterix says as the trio spend the night at an inn just outside Massilia. 'We don't want any of the food we have collected to go off before we get back to our village!' So they travel on horseback for the next two stages of their journey: first to Tolosa to buy some sausage and then to Aginum to buy some prunes. 'Borrowing' a fresh pair of horses, they are soon setting off for their very last destination: Burdigala on Gaul's west coast. 'All we have to do is keep following this river until it reaches the sea!' Asterix says as he wonders which bank they should favour.

Which will you decide for them?

If river's left bank   **go to 22**
If river's right bank   **go to 3**

146

'I wonder if we were right not to try somewhere else along the beach?' Asterix asks as they find only the tiniest of spaces for themselves here. 'There seem to be more people at this part than grains of sand! Still, I suppose we won't notice once we've closed our eyes . . . ' But the Gauls have barely commenced their sunbathing when a large Roman sandal appears just in front of Asterix's nose. 'You two are the palest on the beach!' a voice barks down at them. 'Is that because you are northerners, because you are the two outlaws we're looking for? Tell me the password at once! Is it sunburn, lobster or sunstroke?

If you have picked up the PASSWORD SCROLL during the adventure, you may use it here to find out the correct password. You do this by placing the scroll exactly over the shape below. If you haven't picked up the SCROLL, you'll have to guess the password.

If you think it's SUNBURN   **go to 38**
If you think it's LOBSTER   **go to 173**
If you think it's SUNSTROKE   **go to 262**

'We'll look for an inn,' Asterix says as they cautiously wander from one street to another. 'I'm sure an innkeeper will be able to tell us which boats can be trusted.' Turning a corner, they in fact spot *three* inns. They seem to have found the town's main square and there's The Ox and Cart on the left side of the square, The Brimming Amphora on the right side and The Peasant's Head at its far side. The Gauls happily approach the inns, little realising that all three currently contain a contingent of Romans (some contingents made up of more patrols than others!) having an afternoon drink . . .

Which inn do you wish them to enter?

If The Ox and Cart	**go to 126**
If The Brimming Amphora	**go to 23**
If The Peasant's Head	**go to 207**

148
THE GAULS
ARE CONFRONTED BY

ROMAN PATROLS HERE

Keep throwing the dice until the Gauls have knocked out this number of patrols. Any magic potions rolled before this total is reached must be deducted from the score on the MAGIC POTION COUNTER. When the Gauls have finished the fight, go to 169.

'At last – Burdigala!' Asterix exclaims as they reach the large port. 'Our journey is nearly over, Obelix,' he tells his friend. 'We should be able to board a merchant ship here that will take us right back to our part of Gaul. But first, we mustn't forget to buy the local speciality. It's oysters!' *Go to 30.*

The Gauls hurry across to the ship being loaded with wine barrels and dash up the gangplank. 'Did you see anyone come on board carrying a large bag over his shoulder?' Asterix frantically asks the ship's captain. The captain strokes his long beard for a moment. 'Was it a *yellow* bag?' he asks thoughtfully. 'With a large patch on it?' Asterix eagerly nods his head. 'No, I didn't,' the captain replies casually. Asterix loses his temper with him, demanding why it was then that he asked if it was yellow and had a large patch! 'Because there's just such a bag down there,' the captain tells him simply. 'Can you see?' *Go to 270.*

151

'Well if you say it's not Fingerlix, how about Klunkklix?' Asterix asks. But unfortunately the captain shakes his head at this name as well. 'So it must be Seniorservix!' Asterix says with a grin of satisfaction. All these guesses of his have aroused the captain's suspicions about him, however. He's now sure that Asterix must be a Roman spy trying to wheedle information out of him! And there's only one thing for Roman spies in the captain's book. Keel-hauling! *Go to 20*.

152

'Didn't you say that this was our very last chance to defeat them?' a dazed soldier asks his even more dazed superior as the Gauls now walk straight out the other side of the Roman camp. 'Didn't you say that it would all be over for us after this?' His superior can only just muster the strength to groan a reply. 'Yes, I did,' he murmurs. 'I'm afraid that's IT now!' The slumped soldier slides a bit further towards the ground. 'Good!' he says as he now completely passes out. *Go to 263*.

153
THE GAULS
ARE CONFRONTED BY

ROMAN PATROLS HERE

Keep throwing the dice until the Gauls have knocked out this

number of patrols. *Any magic potions rolled before this total is reached must be deducted from the score on the MAGIC POTION COUNTER. When the Gauls have finished the fight, go to 260.*

154

'So, non-regulation red trousers AND you get the password wrong!' the centurion roars at Asterix. 'You're no more a sailor than I am!' He turns to Obelix. 'As a true and genuine sailor,' he addresses him, 'I order you to take this man down below and put him in irons. When you spot the next school of sharks swimming past, you're to throw him overboard!' Obelix marches Asterix off, pretending to manhandle him, as the Romans now leave their ship. At least, Asterix *thought* Obelix was just pretending. 'All right, all right, the Romans have gone now!' he snaps as Obelix starts to clamp some leg irons on him. 'There's no need to get carried away!' *Go to 217.*

155

'Well, would you believe it?' the captain turns to his men. 'These two are Asterix and Obelix after all. Their password is correct!' He immediately gives the thief a box on the ears and tells him to

scarper. He then picks up the shopping bag and returns it to
Asterix. 'This is yours, I believe,' he tells him politely. 'You've fully
convinced me that you two *are* the wanted outlaws!' It's only quite a
while after our heroes have left the scene that the captain becomes
vaguely aware that he has forgotten something. Now what is it?
Yes, of course. If those two were the wanted outlaws, he should have
arrested them! ***Go to 48***.

156

'Ah, my first customers of the day!' the owner greets them as, the
following morning, Asterix and Obelix find a sweet shop. He picks
up a wooden scoop, waiting for their order. 'Humbugs!' Obelix
says simply. The owner is very insulted by this, angrily slamming
the scoop on to the counter. 'No, it's *not* humbug!' he insists. 'I tell
you that you *are* my very first customers!' Obelix starts to chuckle at
the misunderstanding, explaining that when he said 'humbugs' he
just meant those little sweets tasting of peppermint. 'Oh, my
mistake, my mistake!' the shopkeeper apologises. 'That's always
happening to me when people ask for humbugs. The strange thing
is that they're the only sweets I sell! Now what colour would you
like – pink and yellow, green and red, or black and white?'

Which do you want them to choose?

If pink and yellow humbugs	**go to 234**
If green and red humbugs	**go to 285**
If black and white humbugs	**go to 123**

'Can we have another go?' Obelix asks meekly, putting on his nicest smile, when the farmer tells them that their answer is wrong. 'No, you most certainly can't!' the farmer replies. 'If your puny little friend really *was* Asterix, then he would have got the answer right first time!' Since meekness doesn't work, Obelix decides to try sheer intimidation, reaching for the farmer's neck again. But Asterix restrains his freind. 'That's enough, Obelix!' he tells him. 'We can't blame him for wanting to be careful with his secrets. If we really *were* Romans, then it would be to the lions for all his friends that he sketched. We'll just have to respect that vigilance and do without his drawings.' *Go to 227*.

158

'Where on earth did *that lot* appear from?' the boat's captain asks, quite stunned, after the Gauls have knocked all the Romans over the side and into the water. 'I'd only popped ashore for a quick tankard at The Jolly Sailor and half the Roman Army seems to have sneaked below deck! And, come to think of it, where did *you two* appear from as well?!' The captain's indignation soon passes, however, as Asterix explains who they are – and the mission that they are on. 'Then welcome aboard, welcome aboard!' the captain exclaims, seizing them eagerly by the hand. 'Enemies of Rome are always friends of mine. I was going to have a little nap first but I'll set sail for Lutetia right away!' *Go to 102*.

THE GAULS
ARE CONFRONTED BY

ROMAN PATROLS HERE

Keep throwing the dice until the Gauls have knocked out this number of patrols. Any magic potions rolled before this total is reached must be deducted from the score on the MAGIC POTION COUNTER. When the Gauls have finished the fight, go to 72.

160

The innkeeper pours the Gauls a large tankard of fermented goats' milk each as they happily survey the scene of dazed and unconscious Romans. 'When I spotted you two through the window, as you were approaching my inn, I did wave to you to attract your attention. I wanted to give you a warning,' the innkeeper explains apologetically, 'but one of the soldiers spotted me. He said that if I didn't stop at once he would report me to the weights and measures people for not filling my tankards properly. What could I do? I would have lost my licence!' Asterix and Obelix perfectly understand the predicament the innkeeper was in, though, and tell him to forget it and think no more about it. 'There is one thing we would like you to think about, though,' Asterix adds, 'and that is, which boat on the river can we trust to give us a safe passage to Lutetia?' The innkeeper is delighted to oblige them with this information and whispers the name of a suitable boat. *Go to 102.*

161

'Well, don't you want to collect their helmets now we've knocked them out?' Asterix asks his friend as he contentedly surveys the heaps of dazed Romans on the galley deck. 'You usually do!' This time, though, Obelix decides to forego that pleasure. 'How sensible of you!' Asterix remarks as he follows him over the side of the galley and back towards their rowing-boat below. 'You're concerned that those other galleys might soon raise anchor and come after us!' Obelix pauses for a moment. 'No, that's not what I'm concerned about,' he says. 'I'm concerned that that nice holidaymaker looking after our boat might be missing our company!' *Go to 40.*

162

'Now just you wait your turn!' the Roman snaps at the Gauls as they burst into the delicatessen. 'I was here first and I'm still trying to decide whether I should buy stuffed or unstuffed olives. What would *you* recommend? Do you think I should get stuffed or not?' Yes, Asterix most definitely *does* think the fussy Roman should get stuffed – and is very tempted to tell him so! But he forces himself to refrain . . . especially since this isn't the Roman they were looking for. They've made a costly mistake. The one with the valuable password scroll would have completely vanished into the crowd by now! *Go to 24*.

163

Feeling somewhat annoyed, the Gauls start to trudge along the road's hard shoulder, looking for an emergency carrier-pigeon roost so they can send for a breakdown chariot. The nearest roost is so far away, however, that they decide they might just as well continue the journey to their next destination on foot! Camaracum is only a few more miles away when they notice that the chariots are suddenly having to slow down and form a queue, which is getting longer by the minute . . . *Go to 283*.

164
THE GAULS
ARE CONFRONTED BY

ROMAN PATROLS HERE

Keep throwing the dice until the Gauls have knocked out this number of patrols. Any magic potions rolled before this total is reached must be deducted from the score on the MAGIC POTION COUNTER. When the Gauls have finished the fight, go to 35.

'I rather wish we had just bundled all the Romans into their own guard tower and locked the door,' Asterix says as their chariot resumes its journey across the bridge. 'I feel a bit guilty about tossing them all into the water,' he adds pensively. Obelix finds this hard to understand, though. It was a lot more fun hurling them into the water . . . and it's not as if any of the Romans couldn't swim. 'Oh, it's not the Romans that I feel guilty about,' Asterix explains. 'It's the river. There's enough pollution of the waterways these days, without us adding to it!' *Go to 137.*

Unfortunately, Rotomagus proves much further than Asterix was hoping and it becomes clear that they won't reach it before nightfall. 'We'll knock at one of those three farmers' huts down there,' he says, pointing into the dusky valley beneath them. 'When we explain who we are, I'm sure they won't mind giving us a bed for the night.' What Asterix doesn't realise, though, is that the leader of the nearby Roman garrison, Cleverdickus, had *anticipated* that the

Gauls would have to spend the night there. The farmers' huts are the only dwellings for miles! He'd therefore tried to bribe each of the farmers, asking them to hide some Roman patrols in their huts. Sadly, only *one* of the farmers refused to accept the bribe, driving the Romans away from his property with his geese!

Which hut in the valley would you like the Gauls to call at?

    If hut with one smoking chimney   **go to 114**
    If hut with two smoking chimneys   **go to 2**
    If hut with no smoking chimneys   **go to 259**

167

The Gauls rise so early the next morning that finding an unattended chariot proves no problem for them. What *might* prove a problem, though, is the main road down to Nicae. The Mediterranean town is a popular holiday resort and there might be bad traffic jams. Should they risk this main road – or would they do better to take a longer but less busy *country* road?

Which do you want them to choose?

    If the main road   **go to 238**
    If a country road   **go to 11**

Back on the road again, our heroes at last reach Nicae. 'The first thing *I'm* going to do,' Asterix exclaims as he leaps down from their chariot and massages his stiff neck, 'is do a nice bit of sunbathing on the beach. After all those hours of bad-tempered cart-drivers thumping on their oxen horns at me, I feel I deserve it!' Obelix and Dogmatix secretly exchange ironic glances. The most bad-tempered driver of them all had been Asterix himself! *Go to 241*.

'You see, *you* got off lightly!' Asterix addresses the tied-up driver in the back of the cart after he and Obelix have knocked out all the soldiers at the roadblock. 'So stop complaining!' he adds as the cart starts to jolt the poor wretch from side to side again. When the Gauls finally reach Lugdunum, they check that the Roman isn't too bruised. All things considered, he's in remarkably good condition. 'So that advice from the post office is right,' Asterix chuckles as they release him. 'If you don't want your packages to be damaged, always make sure that they are wrapped and tied *securely*!' *Go to 218*.

'You two do realise that pirates are often encountered on this route?' the ship's captain warns the Gauls after they have set sail. 'And sometimes even Roman galleys. Perhaps whole fleets of them!' Obelix gleefully rubs his hands at this prospect – but Asterix's gaze has suddenly become intent on the captain's bushy

beard and shaved head. He was sure that the farmer had said that the Resistance leader in these waters possessed features just like these! If only Asterix could recall the *name* the farmer gave them. Which was it; Seniorservix, Klunkklix or Fingerlix?

If you have picked up the SKETCHPAD during the adventure, you may consult it here to find out the captain's name. If not, you'll have to guess which of the three possibilities Asterix should give.

If you prefer SENIORSERVIX　　**go to 202**
If you prefer KLUNKKLIX　　**go to 44**
If you prefer FINGERLIX　　**go to 151**

'Just as I suspected!' the Roman captain bawls at them. 'You're not fishermen at all. You're those two Gauls! Put them in chains, men!' So, before they know it, Asterix and Obelix are securely manacled.

They are then dragged through the town in a very rough manner behind the soldiers. 'Do you think this means that your guess at the password was wrong?' Obelix asks innocently. But Asterix is too busy trying to slip a hand free from his chains . . . *Go to 42*.

Go to 42

172
THE GAULS
ARE CONFRONTED BY

ROMAN PATROLS HERE

Keep throwing the dice until the Gauls have knocked out this number of patrols. Any magic potions rolled before this total is reached must be deducted from the score on the MAGIC POTION COUNTER. When the Gauls have finished the fight, go to 79.

173
'Well, I don't deny that it was only a guess,' Asterix says nonchalantly when the Roman tells him that his password was wrong. 'I didn't say we *were* from round here, did I? We happen to be on our holidays if that's all right with you!' The Roman is still not sure about them, though. 'Let's see your suntan lotion, then!' he challenges them. Asterix thinks quickly, uncorks his gourd of magic potion and cheekily offers it to the Roman for his skinny white legs. The Gauls fall about laughing as he walks off in a huff! Unfortunately, though, Asterix forgets to return the cork to his

gourd. He only realises an hour later . . . and by that time some of it has evaporated in the heat!

Reduce MAGIC POTION by 1 measure. Go next to 241.

174

It's been such a long, tiring day that Asterix suggests they pop into a quayside tavern for a refreshing goblet of goats' milk each. 'Any bar snacks with your drinks?' the tavern keeper asks as he reaches for an amphora of goats' milk. 'Yes, please,' Obelix replies before Asterix can stop him, 'could we have a little dish of nuts, a little dish of olives and a little dish of whole wild boar. A dozen will do.' Asterix has a slightly worried look as he watches his friend tuck in to these snacks. And an even more worried look when they receive the bill. It's nineteen gold coins!

If you have picked up the COINBAG during the adventure, you can use this to pay the tavern keeper. Rotate the disc to 'count out' the 19 gold coins – then go to the number that appears on the other side of the card. If you don't have the COINBAG, go to 244 instead.

Clever Dogmatix! Asterix realises that the man exactly fits the farmer's description of the Resistance leader here. Now what did

the farmer say his name was? Asterix is sure it was either Spongemix, Chokkybix or Nosepix!

If you have picked up the SKETCHPAD during the adventure, you may consult it here to find out the man's name. If not, you'll have to guess which of the three possibilities Asterix should give.

If you prefer SPONGEMIX	**go to 200**
If you prefer CHOKKYBIX	**go to 28**
If you prefer NOSEPIX	**go to 91**

When the bowls player tells him that Spongemix isn't his name, Asterix decides to have another guess. But then he notices a patrol of Romans hurrying towards them from the far end of the quay. 'I've a horrible feeling it's *us* they're after!' Asterix whispers anxiously to his friend. 'We can't spare the time to hang around and fight them. We'd better make a run for it!' Asterix has only dashed a few metres, however, when he suddenly slips on something and tumbles to the ground . . . ***Go to 105***.

'Look at that man, crossing the road!' Asterix tells his friend excitedly. 'He seems to fit the farmer's description of the Resistance leader here! I'm sure *he* will direct us to a butcher.' But when they

stop the man, the Gauls find him not nearly as helpful as they'd hoped. He's highly suspicious, thinking that they might be Romans trying to lure him into a trap. 'I might be a Resistance leader, I might not,' he tells them cagily. 'You'll only find out if you can tell me what my name is. I don't answer to anyone who can't!' Asterix and Obelix desperately scratch their heads. They were sure that the farmer had given the Lutetian Resistance leader's name as either Klunkklix, Compactdix or Freekix. The problem is–*which*?

If you have picked up the SKETCHPAD during the adventure, you may consult it here to find out this person's name. If not, you'll have to guess which of the three possibilities Asterix should give.

If you prefer KLUNKKLIX   **go to 255**
If you prefer COMPACTDIX   **go to 84**
If you prefer FREEKIX   **go to 135**

178
THE GAULS
ARE CONFRONTED BY

ROMAN PATROLS HERE

Keep throwing the dice until the Gauls have knocked out this number of patrols. Any magic potions rolled before this total is reached must be deducted from the score on the MAGIC POTION COUNTER. When the Gauls have finished the fight, go to 258.

179

'If you two are fishermen, how come you don't smell of fish?' the captain demands, drawing his sword. Asterix remains calm, though. 'That doesn't mean anything,' he replies simply. 'I could equally well ask more or less the same of you. Given that you're *not* a fisherman, how come you *do* smell of fish?' The captain immediately starts to blush with shame. Has he got B.O. . . . why haven't any of his men ever told him . . . is that why he has never been promoted higher than captain? It's only after several minutes of this excruciating self-doubt that he suddenly realises that he has been tricked. But by then the Gauls are far away! *Go to 145.*

180

'Aren't there any more?' Obelix asks disappointedly as he glances round at all the Romans they have knocked out. There are some lying on the ground, some lying in the bushes and even one or two half-way up a tree! 'No there aren't!' Asterix scowls at him as he dusts down his hands. 'Even those were more than enough. You seem to have forgotten that Getafix instructed us to try to *avoid* Romans on this mission – not walk right into the middle of them!' Obelix starts to sulk, sheepishly looking down at his feet. 'But I don't suppose we'll be able to avoid them *all the time*!' Asterix adds with a grin, immediately cheering up his friend. *Go to 25.*

181

'I thought cowsheds were meant to be for *cows*,' Obelix says as they continue their gallop along this detour path. 'What were all those Romans doing in there?' he adds, somewhat bewildered. Asterix considers this for a moment. 'I suppose it was meant to be an ambush,' he replies casually. 'Oh, I see what the idea was!' Obelix exclaims brightly as it suddenly dawns on him. 'They were to hide in the cowsheds and then when we came innocently galloping past, they were to leap out and overwhelm us! It was quite a clever idea really, wasn't it? A shame in a way that it was such a complete failure!' *Go to 149.*

182

The waiter immediately leads the Gauls into the inn's kitchens. 'There's the other Asterix!' he says, pointing to a quivering wretch in the corner. 'What a fool I've been!' he adds apologetically. 'This impostor told me he was you and since he had this bag of regional specialities with him I believed him and told him he could hide down here.' The wretch starts to plead for mercy as the two Gauls menacingly approach him. 'Don't worry,' Asterix says sternly as he snatches their shopping bag back from the thief. 'I haven't got time to give you a good drubbing. But I *have* just got time to give you a home truth. You and your ugly face don't look A BIT like me!' ***Go to 48***.

183
'Why were all those Romans hiding up in the trees like that?' Obelix asks casually as he and Asterix resume their gallop through the wood. Asterix brushes a few leaves from his shirt. 'I think it was meant to be an ambush,' he says. 'That's probably why they suddenly jumped down on us. Or perhaps they just like it up in the trees. It certainly didn't take long before they were back up there again! Mind you,' he adds with a chuckle, 'it was with a little help from our fists . . . ' ***Go to 149***.

184
'Well, was a gold bangle the right answer or not?' Asterix asks impatiently. 'Er . . . yes, yes, of course it was,' the farmer replies, although his sheepishness clearly gives away that it wasn't. He

obviously doesn't want Obelix throttling him again! 'I'll start the sketches right away,' he continues. 'Let me just finish milking Buttergoblet here. Oh dear, I've just pulled a muscle!' he suddenly adds. 'Mine, I mean, not hers. It's in my sketching arm too. I'm afraid I won't be able to help you after all!' Asterix isn't at all taken in by this excuse, of course, but there is little he can do about it. Obelix can throttle the farmer until his cows come home but he can't actually *force* him to do the sketches. Not accurate ones at any rate! So Asterix decides that they'll just have to continue their journey without them. *Go to 227.*

185
THE GAULS
ARE CONFRONTED BY

ROMAN PATROLS HERE

Keep throwing the dice until the Gauls have knocked out this number of patrols. Any magic potions rolled before this total is reached must be deducted from the score on the MAGIC POTION COUNTER. When the Gauls have finished the fight, go to 269.

186

'I wish you hadn't hit them quite so hard on this occasion,' Asterix complains to his friend when all the Romans are floundering in the water below them. Obelix is a little worried by Asterix's comment. Surely he's not starting to feel compassion for those horrible

Romans? Surely he's not actually going *soft* in his old age? But Asterix soon puts his fears at rest. 'You hit them so hard,' he continues irritably, 'that when they splashed into the water the decks were completely swamped. You could have sunk the boat!' So, for once Obelix doesn't mind his friend's grumpiness. In fact, as they now set sail for Lutetia, he seems rather pleased by it! ***Go to 102.***

187

'Are we absolutely sure that's our Roman?' Asterix asks, starting to have doubts, as they follow him along the street. 'Perhaps he'd gone behind that curtain to take an outfit *off*, not to put one *on*. Perhaps he really *is* a senator!' But at that moment a roll of parchment suddenly slips down from under the senator's toga. Dogmatix immediately scampers forward to pick it up before a passer-by can get it and hand it back to the Roman. 'Well done, Dogmatix!' Asterix says, beaming at the little dog as he takes the roll of parchment from him. 'Look, Obelix – it's the password scroll!'

You are now entitled to use the PASSWORD SCROLL. Go next to 24.

188
THE GAULS
ARE CONFRONTED BY

ROMAN PATROLS HERE

Keep throwing the dice until the Gauls have knocked out this number of patrols. Any magic potions rolled before this total is reached must be deducted from the score on the MAGIC POTION COUNTER. When the Gauls have finished the fight, go to 152.

189

The Gauls haven't walked far along the main road when they again come across an unattended Roman chariot. It's parked in a discreet place just off the road, in front of some thick bushes. 'The driver must be answering a call of nature!' Asterix deduces as they clamber into the chariot. 'Look, this one's drawn by *two* horses. We should reach Durocortorum in no time!' *Go to 74.*

'A large pot of your fish stew, please,' Asterix says to the skinny red-haired woman when they have walked up to her stall. 'And tie the lid down as tightly as you can,' he adds. 'It's got a long way to travel!' Asterix should have been a bit more discreet, though – a passing Roman overhears this last remark. Remembering that he was ordered to be on the lookout for two travellers from the very north of Gaul, the soldier immediately challenges our heroes . . . *Go to 111*.

'Right – seize them, men!' the captain barks. 'They got the password wrong!' Seeing no alternative but to fight, Asterix immediately uncorks his gourd of magic potion. But then, before he takes a swig, he *does* see an alternative. He notices a large sack of very round humbugs in the corner and he hurls a handful at the Romans' feet as they come charging towards him. The Romans go sliding all over the place and crashing to the floor! But as the chuckling Gauls make their getaway from the shop, Asterix realises that he might just as well have used his magic potion after all. There's a large damp patch on his shirt – in his excitement, he must have spilt some of the potion!

Reduce MAGIC POTION by 1 measure. Go next to 257.

192

'You might have hit on the right code once, but not twice!' the shopkeeper says as he hands them their box of humbugs. 'You'll find the bag of gold coins hidden underneath the sweets,' he adds. 'Guard it with your lives. The freedom fighters are in much need of it.' Hearing this, Asterix feels that he has to confess that they're *not* the go-betweens. He explains who they *really* are. 'Asterix and Obelix! What an honour!' the shopkeeper exclaims, proudly shaking their hands. 'Well, I insist that you take the bag of gold coins anyway. Important though the cause of the freedom fighters is, I'm sure they would agree that yours is even more so!'

You are now entitled to use the COINBAG CARD. Go next to 257.

193

Asterix insists to the Roman that they *are* locals, though. It's just that this is the first time that they have been able to afford this special wine! 'Hum?' the Roman considers, still rather doubtful about them. 'Well, give me the town password. Is it champagne, bubbly or champers?'

If you have picked up the PASSWORD SCROLL during the

adventure, you may use it here to find out the correct password. You do this by placing the SCROLL exactly over the shape below. If you haven't picked up the SCROLL, you'll have to guess the password.

If you think it's CHAMPAGNE   **go to 100**
If you think it's BUBBLY   **go to 237**
If you think it's CHAMPERS   **go to 225**

194

Asterix was right in thinking that the second-class cart wouldn't be searched at any of the roadblocks they encountered. The Romans there obviously thought that no one would be mad enough to hide in a cart as slow and bumpy as this one. And, after two aching nights and days of being curled up in the mail-bags, Asterix himself is beginning to think that they must be mad! Anyway, at least they had avoided a confrontation with the Romans. But for how long? For, as they quickly become lost in the narrow, maze-like streets of Lugdunum, Asterix gets the distinct feeling that they have walked into a trap! 'I'm sure there's an ambush waiting for us down at least one of these alleys,' he remarks anxiously as he wonders which one they should take next . . .

Which will you choose for them?

If alley running north   **go to 214**
If alley running east   **go to 60**
If alley running south   **go to 273**
If alley running west   **go to 159**

195

The poor holidaymaker's eyes nearly pop out of his head as he sees the two Gauls scrambling back down the side of the galley. Were all those thumps he'd heard *theirs*? And were all the yells and hollers *the*

Romans? 'Don't worry, we're perfectly all right,' Asterix reassures him as he and Obelix leap back into the rowing-boat. 'Thanks for minding Dogmatix for us!' But the holidaymaker *wasn't* worried about them. In fact, he was rather hoping that the two Gauls *wouldn't* be all right. Then perhaps he might have been able to have the rowing-boat to himself again! ***Go to 40***.

196
THE GAULS
ARE CONFRONTED BY

ROMAN PATROLS HERE

Keep throwing the dice until the Gauls have knocked out this number of patrols. Any magic potions rolled before this total is reached must be deducted from the score on the MAGIC POTION COUNTER. When the Gauls have finished the fight, go to 158.

197

'No payment, no stew!' the woman insists, yanking the pot back from them – but then she notices the little gourd at Asterix's hip. 'Is that a flask of brandy you've got there?' she asks eagerly. 'I'll tell you what – you can have the stew for a little nip of that brandy. It helps give me courage to deal with them Romans. You wouldn't believe the cheek some of those boys give me!' Asterix agrees that it is a fair deal and pours the woman a measure of his potion. He feels that he is only *slightly* deceiving her. After all, it will achieve the effect she wants. Although he has to admit, she'll be getting more than just a little nip. And so will those Romans!

Reduce MAGIC POTION by 1 measure. Go next to 236.

198

''Ere, what's your game?' the holidaymaker yells at them when the Gauls have swum out to his rowing-boat and started to haul themselves into it. 'Hijack!' Obelix explains simply, taking over the oars. 'My name isn't Jack, it's Jacques!' the holidaymaker protests. 'Jacques Seasix. And I'm not saying "hi" back to you until you tell me where we're going!' The answer, unfortunately, is . . . ***Go to 113.***

199

As soon as Obelix has returned him to his milking stool, the farmer reveals the names of all the other resistance leaders round Gaul. 'Our man in Lutetia is Compactdix,' he begins proudly. 'You'll recognise him by the vertical stripes on his shirt. In Camaracum it's Klunkklix. He has a checked shirt. In Durocortorum just look for

an innkeeper with a very red nose. His name is Freekix . . . '
Asterix and Obelix try desperately to memorise all these names and
descriptions but it becomes harder and harder as the list goes on. 'I
know what will make it a lot easier for you!' the farmer says,
suddenly having an idea. ***Go to 29.***

200

'No, my name isn't Spongemix!' the man snaps at Asterix. 'Now
keep that dog of yours out of my boat because I'm about to make a
long voyage. It's going to be hard enough rowing myself, without
some scruffy dog as well!' Asterix wonders about the *purpose* of this
long voyage of his, sure that it will have something to do with his
secret job as local Resistance leader. Then he notices a long, bumpy
canvas sheet at one end of the man's boat. No wonder his voyage is
going to be so strenuous. Asterix is sure there's a pile of spears under
that sheet! ***Go to 243.***

201

'No, my name *isn't* Seniorservix,' the busy waiter snaps at Asterix.
'And keep that dog of yours away from that kitchen door over there.
You'll have the Health Inspector on to us!' Dogmatix's nose is
already pushing through the door, however, and there's soon an
excited yapping from him. Racing into the kitchen area themselves, the Gauls spot several sacks of vegetables in the corner. And

cowering behind the sacks is the thief with their shopping bag! 'I know it's a bit of a waste for just one piffling wretch,' Asterix says as he quickly downs a measure of his magic potion before advancing on the thief, 'but after all the trouble he's caused us I think he deserves it, don't you?'

Reduce MAGIC POTION by 1 measure. Go next to 48.

202

'Yes, my hearties!' the captain responds, his beard widening into a broad grin. 'Seniorservix is me! So you two must be Asterix and Obelix! Well, I'll be blowed! Shiver me timbers!' The captain's expression then becomes a lot more anxious, however. 'Don't think that your perils are over yet, shipmates,' he warns them gravely. 'Information has come my way that those scurvy Romans have one *final* ambush prepared for you. But the exact detail isn't certain, I'm afraid. All we have been able to find out is that you shouldn't *take things at face value.* If you do, you'll end up not back in your village but right in the middle of one of the Romans' fortified camps!' *Go to 217.*

203
THE GAULS
ARE CONFRONTED BY

ROMAN PATROLS HERE

Keep throwing the dice until the Gauls have knocked out this

number of patrols. Any magic potions rolled before this total is reached must be deducted from the score on the MAGIC POTION COUNTER. When the Gauls have finished the fight, go to 33.

204

'Any last request?' the captain asks Asterix when his cut-throat crew have placed him on a plank overhanging the side of the ship. 'Yes, just a drop of my liquid comfort here,' Asterix says, reaching for his gourd of magic potion. 'It will make it a little easier for me.' He waves Obelix and Dogmatix goodbye as the bloodthirsty crew force him towards the end of the plank and then push him off with their cutlasses. Immediately, the sharks come swimming towards our hero. But one by one they are sent flying into the air! 'Er . . . sh-shall we just forget about that fare of yours?' the captain stammers when Asterix is soon climbing back on to the ship.

Reduce MAGIC POTION by 1 measure. Go next to 217.

205

The butcher is so slow in wrapping the ham, though, that the Roman is well down the street by the time the Gauls have left the shop. 'I think that's him just entering the wine shop,' says Asterix, peering through the crowds. But Obelix insists it's the one entering the novelty shop. Or is it the one who just disappeared into the delicatessen?

Which of the three shops would you like them to hurry towards?

If wine shop	**go to 230**
If novelty shop	**go to 37**
If delicatessen	**go to 162**

206

'You don't think there will be any ambushes in these bushes, do you?' Asterix asks with a little concern as the Gauls follow the middle path through the wood. But this route is perfectly safe – it is along the other two paths that the Romans are hiding! 'I reckon Asterix has lost his bottle!' the leader of one of the patrols whispers to his men after they have waited and waited. One of these men – a goofy one with large sticking-out ears – doesn't quite understand. 'Or maybe he didn't push the cork into the bottle tightly enough,' he suggests, 'and the magic potion just leaked out!' *Go to 25.*

THE GAULS
ARE CONFRONTED BY

ROMAN PATROLS HERE

Keep throwing the dice until the Gauls have knocked out this number of patrols. Any magic potions rolled before this total is reached must be deducted from the score on the MAGIC POTION COUNTER. When the Gauls have finished the fight, go to 56.

208

Making their way down to the right side of the bridge, the Gauls hide behind some bushes so they can stealthily scrutinise the boats moored there. Three of them look ready to set sail but Asterix is concerned that they might all be hiding a contingent of Romans below deck. 'We're going to have to get a little closer,' he whispers to his overgrown friend. 'Come on, off with your shoes. We're going for a little swim!' *Go to 87.*

209

'Can't I just give this half-unconscious Roman one more thump so he's *totally* unconscious?' Obelix pleads as Asterix tries to drag his friend away from the scene of the punch-up. 'I don't like to leave a job half-finished!' he adds. But Asterix insists that they press on with their journey. 'We must get to Camaracum as quickly as possible or we're likely to lose our way,' he says urgently, glancing up at the sky. 'Look, it's growing dark already. If we're not careful, those Romans stretched out there won't be the only ones seeing stars!' *Go to 101.*

210

When the shopkeeper tells him that Spongemix is wrong, Asterix insists that it's just his bad memory at fault. He decides that he'd better explain exactly who he is. 'You're the famous Asterix?' the shopkeeper scoffs. 'Asterix of the superhuman strength? All right, let's see you lift that cart-full of cabbages out there as proof. If you can, I'll tell you which inns in Camaracum are safe for you and where they'll be happy to give you free food and drink!' Asterix is able to lift the cart quite easily, of course. But only by downing a measure of his magic potion first!

Reduce MAGIC POTION by 1 measure. Go next to 257.

211

The Gauls haven't strolled very far from the fish stall when they walk right into a patrol of Romans. 'Let's see if I can try and *talk* our way out first,' Asterix whispers as Obelix starts to polish his fists. So when the soldiers' captain suspiciously asks who they are and where they're going, Asterix replies that they are merely local fishermen traipsing back to their homes after a long day at sea. 'I don't believe you!' the captain roars. 'Tell me the correct password for the town immediately! Is it squid, octopus or seaweed?

If you have picked up the PASSWORD SCROLL during the adventure, you may use it here to find out the correct password. You do this by placing the SCROLL exactly over the shape below. If you haven't picked up the SCROLL, you'll have to guess the password.

If you think it's SQUID	**go to 94**
If you think it's OCTOPUS	**go to 171**
If you think it's SEAWEED	**go to 246**

'All right, I admit it – we don't live here!' Asterix tells the captain when he is brusquely informed that the password he has given is wrong. 'We are travelling salesmen,' he says. 'We have come with a sample of our spa water to see if this good man will sell it in his shop.' To prove it, he uncorks his gourd of magic potion and persuades the shopkeeper to try a measure. 'Delicious, isn't it?' he asks. 'Oh dear,' he adds, 'did I hear those Romans call you a simpleton? Why don't you show them just what you're made of?' And with the potion already taking effect in his veins, the shopkeeper starts to do just that . . . 'I know it's a shame to let someone else have the pleasure of bashing those Romans,' Asterix chuckles as they make their getaway from the shop, 'but we just don't have the time ourselves!'

Reduce MAGIC POTION by 1 measure. Go next to 257.

213
THE GAULS
ARE CONFRONTED BY

ROMAN PATROLS HERE

Keep throwing the dice until the Gauls have knocked out this number of patrols. Any magic potions rolled before this total is reached must be deducted from the score on the MAGIC POTION COUNTER. When the Gauls have finished the fight, go to 235.

'Did I see a movement amongst those shadows ahead?' Asterix asks anxiously as they follow this alley. Dogmatix starts to growl – and Obelix to polish his knuckles! 'Oh, it's just my imagination,' Asterix says, breathing a sigh of relief as they reach the shadows. 'There's not an ambush here after all.' In actual fact, there was *meant* to be an ambush at this particular corner. But the contingent of Romans instructed to go there found the narrow streets just as confusing as the Gauls. They are currently lying in wait right over on the other side of town! ***Go to 218.***

'Yes, of course we can stop at an inn,' the cart-driver agrees innocently. 'There are four nice little places coming up soon. There's The Running Boar, The Crashing Boar, The Merry Ox and The Crushed Grape. Just let me know which one you would like to pull up at.' As they approach the inns, the cart-driver has an evil snigger to himself. There's a number of Roman patrols hiding in each cellar! The Gauls do have a *slight* chance of avoiding a punch-up, though. The Romans in one of these inns have drunk so much ale while they have been waiting for the Gauls that they are 'knocked out' already!

Will you be fortunate enough to pick this inn for the Gauls to stop at?

If you choose The Running Boar	**go to 103**
If you choose The Crashing Boar	**go to 232**
If you choose The Merry Ox	**go to 153**
If you choose The Crushed Grape	**go to 47**

216

'*There* are a few more Romans answering the call of nature!' Asterix says as the last of the soldiers is sent flying off the bridge and into the muddy water below. 'First they seem to think that they're birds,' he chuckles, 'and then fish!' With the guard tower now deserted, Asterix lifts the heavy barrier there so that their chariot can continue its progress across the bridge. 'What do you mean, they think that they are fish?' Obelix asks quite a few miles later. 'You mean their silvery-plated armour looks like fish scales?' Asterix can only sigh in despair . . . ***Go to 137.***

Our heroes finally reach the port just south of their village. 'Only a few hours to go,' Asterix says joyfully as the trio immediately start to walk the twenty miles or so remaining of their epic journey, 'and we'll be back home. We've SURVIVED all the Roman ambushes and traps!' But on reaching a signpost at a crossroads a few miles further on, Asterix begins to wonder if he might have spoken too soon. The signpost is very loose in the ground – as if someone has twisted it round! 'It says that for our village we should take the path to the right,' Asterix remarks suspiciously, 'but I wonder if those devious Romans have tampered with it? Maybe we should follow one of those other arms of the signpost instead. I realise they point to the Roman camps of Compendium, Laudanum and Aquarium, but perhaps that's deliberately to mislead us!'

Which arm of the signpost do you want them to follow?

If arm that reads COMPENDIUM	**go to 188**
If arm that reads LAUDANUM	**go to 92**
If arm that reads AQUARIUM	**go to 239**
If arm that reads GAULISH VILLAGE	**go to 18**

218

'At last – a proper bed!' Asterix exclaims as they spend the night at a cosy rest-house in Lugdunum. 'And at last – a full tummy!' Obelix responds, patting the hearty roast boar supper inside him. 'Which reminds me,' he adds, 'what is the speciality here? I don't suppose it's boar *this* time?' Asterix has to disappoint him again. 'But you're getting closer,' he laughs. 'It's meatballs. We'll buy some first thing tomorrow and then it's off to Nicae for us, right in the south of Gaul. We'll have to see if we can pinch another chariot from somewhere!' *Go to 167.*

219
THE GAULS
ARE CONFRONTED BY

ROMAN PATROLS HERE

Keep throwing the dice until the Gauls have knocked out this number of patrols. Any magic potions rolled before this total is reached must be deducted from the score on the MAGIC POTION COUNTER. When the Gauls have finished the fight, go to 274.

220

'What were all those Romans doing there?' Obelix asks, bewildered, after the last one has been pummelled into the ground. 'First they were hiding behind some trees and then they weren't!' Asterix scratches his head for a moment before they resume their pleasant stroll along the mountain path. 'I think it was meant to be an ambush,' he replies. 'It certainly had all the classic features of an ambush. The waiting on a bend . . . the hiding behind some trees . . . the sudden jumping out. Yes, I'd definitely say it was meant to be an ambush!' *Go to 40.*

The Romans on this galley are so busy sunbathing, however, that the little rowing-boat is able to creep right past it! The Gauls can't believe their luck. At least, *Asterix* can't believe his luck. *Obelix* doesn't really regard it as lucky. And nor does the poor holiday-maker! He was secretly hoping the Gauls would be put in chains by the Romans so he could have his boat to himself again. But now, it seems, he is stuck with them for *Jupiter knows* how long! ***Go to 40***.

'I hope you'll forgive this little misunderstanding,' the soldier says with embarrassment after he has admitted that their password is correct. 'It's just that, if you don't mind my saying, you don't really *look* like a bullfighter. I've always imagined that they would have to be a lot burlier for a dangerous job like that!' Asterix acts as if this is quite a common misconception. 'Oh no!' he chuckles amiably. 'The most important requirement for a bullfighter is to be very nimble on your feet. So the smaller and lighter the better!' With horror, though, he suddenly realises that he'd said Obelix was a bullfighter as well. By no stretch of the imagination does *he* look nimble on his feet! But, fortunately, the Roman is as gullible as Obelix is fat. Perfectly satisfied about them, he wishes them good-day! ***Go to 174***.

223

The Gauls search the ship from top to bottom. They look behind crates, between crates and inside crates. 'This is *crating* on my nerves!' Asterix says frantically. 'We've obviously chosen the wrong ship. The thief and our bag are nowhere to be found.' But Obelix is for the moment more concerned about Dogmatix. *He* is nowhere to be found either! But suddenly they hear him yapping in the distance, on the ship being loaded with baskets . . . followed by a yell and a splash. A few moments later they see Dogmatix slowly descending the ship's gangplank – *slowly* because he is dragging the shopping bag behind him! 'He must have picked up the scent of those sausages in the bag,' Obelix says proudly. 'And then *sent* the thief into the water!' *Go to 86*.

224
THE GAULS
ARE CONFRONTED BY

ROMAN PATROLS HERE

Keep throwing the dice until the Gauls have knocked out this

number of patrols. Any magic potions rolled before this total is reached must be deducted from the score on the MAGIC POTION COUNTER. When the Gauls have finished the fight, go to 8.

225

'Champers is correct,' the Roman tells them. 'My apologies to you, O townspeople. You're not the two outlaws after all!' He feels so bad about his mistake that he indulges in a little sociable conversation with them. 'May I ask what the special occasion *is* that you're buying the fizzy wine for?' he enquires. It's Obelix who is the quickest to reply. 'Yes, it's for a banquet to humiliate the Romans,' he answers affably. 'I'm sure you'll agree that you can't get a more special –' But he isn't allowed to finish his sentence. Asterix grabs him by one of his pigtails and tugs him quickly away from there! *Go to 261.*

226

The captain strokes his chin as he thoughtfully studies Obelix. Yes, he does look rather overweight . . . and he most *definitely* does look simple! So he decides to risk it and turns back to Asterix. 'All right,' the captain addresses him, 'if *you* are the wanted outlaws from the north-west of Gaul, then you should be able to tell me the correct password for that region. Is it bother, nuisance or irritation?'

If you have picked up the PASSWORD SCROLL during the adventure, you may consult it here to find out the correct password. You do this by placing the SCROLL exactly over the shape below. If you haven't picked up the SCROLL, you'll have to guess the password.

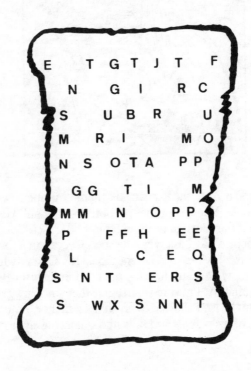

If you think it's BOTHER   **go to 155**
If you think it's NUISANCE   **go to 264**
If you think it's IRRITATION   **go to 89**

The trio have walked a good few miles from the farmer when Asterix suddenly realises that they didn't find out from him whether this is the right direction for Lutetia or not! However, they eventually arrive at a signpost which reads ROTOMAGUS. 'Rotomagus? Rotomagus?' Asterix says to himself, stroking his chin. 'Ah, I know where that is! It's down river from Lutetia, about fifty miles to the north. We'll board a boat there and sail the rest of the way to Lutetia. It will save our feet!' ***Go to 166***.

WE'LL BOARD A BOAT THERE FOR LUTETIA.

After our heroes have sent all the Romans flying over the side of the boat into the water (oh, all except one that is – who ended up doubled over one of the yard-arms!), Dogmatix discovers something very curious below deck. There's someone there in his underwear, securely bound hand and foot! 'I'm the boat's real captain,' he explains as soon as Asterix has removed the apple stuffed into his mouth. 'That one above who welcomed you aboard was really a Roman centurion who'd pinched my clothes!' Asterix chuckles as he recalls that other captain plunging head first into the water. 'Well, at least your clothes will have had a good clean!' he tells him. 'I'll make a deal with you. I'll get your clothes back for you, beautifully washed, and you take us to Lutetia!' ***Go to 102***.

229

'Are we on the right track for Lutetia?' Asterix asks politely as the two friends approach the farmer. 'My name is Asterix and I'm on a mission to travel right round occupied Gaul.' The farmer starts to laugh through his long, unkempt moustache as he pulls at the cow's udder. 'Pull the *udder* one!' he chortles. 'Puny little you *Asterix*? Asterix the famous scourge of Rome? What do you take me for?' Obelix doesn't like his little friend being laughed at, though, and immediately lifts the farmer off the ground by the scruff of his neck. 'All right, all right, he *is* Asterix!' the poor farmer splutters. 'And if you let me down I can help you. I'm the leader of the local Gaulish Resistance here!' ***Go to 199***.

230

The Gauls burst into the wine shop . . . but the Roman being served there isn't the one they're looking for. His nose is a lot more bulbous! 'The trouble with these Romans is that they all look the same from the back,' Asterix grumbles as the disappointed trio leave the shop. Obelix nods his head in agreement. 'Yes, they all look the same when they've been thumped as well,' he adds thoughtfully. 'They always seem to have the same vacant eyes for some reason – and the same drooping tongues.' *Go to 24*.

231

'It's obviously *us* they're looking for at the roadblocks!' Asterix remarks with concern. 'If we had a decent horse we could try rushing one of them but we won't stand a chance with this useless animal. We're just going to have to get out there and fight the Romans. I wonder which of the two roadblocks has the *fewest* soldiers manning it?'

Which roadblock do you want the Gauls to approach?

If the one in the slow lane	**go to 138**
If the one in the fast lane	**go to 219**

232
THE GAULS
ARE CONFRONTED BY

ROMAN PATROLS HERE

Keep throwing the dice until the Gauls have knocked out this number of patrols. Any magic potions rolled before this total is reached must be deducted from the score on the MAGIC POTION COUNTER. When the Gauls have finished the fight, go to 99.

As soon as they have tossed all the Romans off the bridge, Asterix lifts the heavy barrier so their chariot can continue on its journey. But the little Gaul can't resist one last glance at all the soldiers spluttering in the water. 'If only they could fight as well as they can dive!' he jokes to Obelix. 'I've never seen such impressive triple spins and back-flips. I admit their entry into the water is sometimes a bit cumbersome but their flight through the air is a real joy to behold!' *Go to 137.*

The two friends are just leaving the shop with their little basket of pink and yellow humbugs when Asterix suddenly stops. He turns round to have another look at the shopkeeper. Now why does that distinctive checked shirt he's wearing seem to ring a bell? Yes, that's it! Hadn't that farmer described just such a shirt – belonging to one of the Resistance leaders! *Go to 13.*

'Wasn't that thoughtful of them, Asterix?' Obelix says, smiling as the last of the Romans goes sailing high into the trees. 'They knew that we might get a bit bored on this lonely track and so they sent a few patrols out to amuse us!' As the two Gauls continue on their way, Obelix soon hears another noise – a loud rustling in the bushes. More Romans? he wonders excitedly. No, it's something even better than that. Wild boar! 'Wasn't that thoughtful of the boar too?' he says contentedly when he later has a couple of them slung over his shoulder. 'They must have known that we would probably get a bit hungry on this lonely track and so a few of them wandered out to feed us!' *Go to 101.*

236

The Gauls haven't walked far from the woman's stall when Obelix notices some locals rolling heavy wooden balls along the quay. He asks his friend what they're doing. 'It's a pavement game that's very popular round here,' Asterix replies. 'It's called *bowls*. The idea is that you try and roll your ball as close to –' But he suddenly breaks off on noticing that one of the players is wearing red spotted

trousers. Didn't that farmer say that the Resistance leader in Massilia had trousers like that? But what did the farmer say his name was? Asterix is sure it was either Chokkybix, Spongemix or Nosepix . . .

If you have picked up the SKETCHPAD during the adventure,

you may consult it here to find out the man's name. If not, you'll
have to guess which of the three possibilities Asterix should give.

If you prefer CHOKKYBIX   **go to 117**
If you prefer SPONGEMIX   **go to 176**
If you prefer NOSEPIX   **go to 279**

237

'Why don't you fizz up one of our bottles and aim it at him!' Asterix
whispers to his friend when the Roman tells them that their
password is wrong and raises his spear at them again. Obelix
slightly misunderstands the instruction, though, and immediately
plucks the gourd of magic potion from Asterix's belt. 'All right, I'm
fizzing it up,' he tells him after he has removed the cork. 'What
happens now?' Asterix quickly grabs the potion back from him.
'What happens now is that you have spilt some of it!' he says
furiously. 'I meant fizz up one of those *wine* bottles in your bag.
Look, I'll show you!' The cork explodes from the bottle and knocks
the Roman for six. Obelix sheepishly agrees that the wine bottle
does work rather better!

Reduce MAGIC POTION by 1 measure. Go next to 261.

'Well, no traffic jams so far,' Asterix comments as they reach the half-way mark for Nicae. 'Let's hope we're in luck!' But it's not much longer before they meet their first traffic jam . . . then their second . . . then their third. 'What's the cause this time?' Asterix screams with exasperation as they encounter the longest jam of all, some twenty milestones from Nicae. 'It's roadworks, can you believe? Fancy doing roadworks right in the middle of the holiday season!' *Go to 288.*

239

'So I was right about that signpost!' Asterix remarks as they spot their village in the distance. 'It *had* been twisted round. How treacherous those Romans are!' As the village gradually comes closer, Obelix gives the occasional sob. 'Yes, I know the feeling, dear friend,' Asterix comforts him. 'There's no sight quite like home sweet home, is there?' Obelix makes a huge effort to hold back one of his sobs for a moment. 'No, that's not what I'm upset about,' he explains. 'It's that signpost being turned round, making us think that we were heading for a Roman camp. I was really looking forward to one last punch-up!' *Go to 263.*

240

Since Asterix doesn't have nine gold coins, he offers to replace all the fish. 'Oh yes, and how are you going to do that?' the woman demands as he gathers up a net and climbs into the nearest fishing-boat. 'There's a whole week's catch here!' But just a few minutes after rowing out of the harbour, Asterix is back again. With the boat crammed full of fish! After the Gauls have bid the stupefied woman goodbye, Asterix has a few cross words for Dogmatix. 'And I don't know why *you* are looking so pleased with yourself!' he chides him. 'Catching all that fish cost me a precious measure of potion!'

Reduce MAGIC POTION by 1 measure. Go next to 211.

241

'We'll sleep here tonight, under the stars,' Asterix says as the crowded beach at last empties and the sun slips slowly down towards the horizon. 'Tomorrow,' he adds sleepily, 'we make our way to Massilia, which is further along the coast. First, though, we must remember to collect the local speciality from Nicae. It's fresh salad!' So the next morning, after they have purchased a large amphora of salad, the Gauls consider how best to travel the short distance to Massilia. They could either go on foot – or hijack one of the holidaymakers' rowing-boats!

Which method will you choose for them?

If go on foot	**go to 12**
If hijack boat	**go to 198**

'You want the best fish stew in town, do you?' the fisherman considers after the Gauls have approached him. 'The fish stew is good everywhere in Massilia. But if you want the very best you should try one of those four quayside stalls over there.' Following the direction of the fisherman's finger, the Gauls see that one stall is served by a plump dark-haired woman; one by a plump red-haired woman; one by a skinny dark-haired woman; and one by a skinny red-haired woman.

Whose stall will you choose for them?

If plump dark-haired woman's	**go to 53**
If plump red-haired woman's	**go to 112**
If skinny dark-haired woman's	**go to 277**
If skinny red-haired woman's	**go to 190**

'It looks as if he's doing a bit of *spear-running*,' Asterix whispers to Obelix. 'He must be delivering the spears to various Resistance members hiding in coves along the coast. It's a very important and dangerous job he's doing. I must try and make it a bit easier for him!' So Asterix immediately uncorks his gourd of magic potion and offers the man a swig. 'Just to show there are no hard feelings about our dog, have a drop of brandy,' he insists. He gives Obelix a little wink as the man gratefully accepts. And a much bigger wink when, just a few seconds later, the man and his boat have completely disappeared from the harbour. They are way out to sea already!

Reduce MAGIC POTION by 1 measure. Go next to 174.

244

When an embarrassed Asterix confesses that they can't settle the bill, the tavern keeper points them towards a little door at the back. 'Then it's into the kitchen for you two!' he orders them furiously. 'You can do the washing-up!' The two Gauls gasp on seeing the stacks and stacks of dirty platters and goblets in the kitchen. The washing-up clearly hasn't been done for weeks! *Go to 119*.

245
THE GAULS
ARE CONFRONTED BY

ROMAN PATROLS HERE

Keep throwing the dice until the Gauls have knocked out this number of patrols. Any magic potions rolled before this total is reached must be deducted from the score on the MAGIC POTION COUNTER. When the Gauls have finished the fight, go to 181.

'Just as I thought!' the captain roars at them. 'You're no more fishermen that I am! You two are Asterix and Obelix, that's who you are. But I suppose you're going to deny it? I suppose you're going to tell me that that gourd at your belt *doesn't* contain a potion that bestows a terrifying strength?' To the captain's surprise, Asterix nonchalantly shakes his head. 'No, I'm not going to deny it,' he replies, immediately uncorking the gourd and putting it to his lips. But when he has gulped down a measure of the potion he finds that the Romans have all fled! 'I just don't understand these Romans,' he sighs. 'They insist that I'm honest with them and when I am they just don't want to know. What an annoying waste of potion!'

Reduce MAGIC POTION by 1 measure. Go next to 145.

247

Asterix quickly downs a measure of his magic potion in readiness for these soldiers. But then the scream comes again . . . and it turns out to be just a spoilt child! 'I said I want my toast cut up into SOLDIERS, not triangles!' he bawls at his harassed parents. Asterix lets out a despairing sigh as he returns the gourd to his belt. What a waste of good potion!

Reduce MAGIC POTION by 1 measure. Go next to 168.

248

So Obelix immediately prepares for a fight himself, clenching his fists. The captain relents and offers them one more chance, though. 'If you aren't lying and really do live here,' he says to them, 'you should be able to tell me the town password. Is it storm, cloud or thunder?'

If you have picked up the PASSWORD SCROLL during the adventure, you may use it here to find out the correct password. You do this by placing the SCROLL exactly over the shape below. If you haven't picked up the scroll, you'll have to guess the password.

If you think it's STORM	**go to 65**
If you think it's CLOUD	**go to 191**
If you think it's THUNDER	**go to 212**

'Swabbie is correct,' the centurion tells Asterix with surprise. 'So you *are* a real swabbie after all!' Asterix is greatly relieved by this but Obelix is feeling rather left out. He runs up to the centurion just as he and his men are leaving the ship. 'Am I a real swabbie as well?' he asks eagerly. The centurion secretly rolls his eyes at one of his men and mockingly taps his finger on his head, as if to say, they've got a real bird-brain here! 'Of course you are, of course you are,' he humours the Gaul. Obelix does a little jig of delight. 'Oh, by the way,' he calls after the centurion as he steps into his little boarding boat below. 'What does a swabbie *mean*?' **Go to 217.**

The Wooden Leg is so full of noise and smoke that working out whether the thief is there or not proves more difficult than the Gauls had hoped! 'Has anyone dashed in here with a yellow bag over his shoulder?' Asterix hurriedly asks at the table nearest the door. The sailor sitting there shakes his head. 'But I did see such a person racing past the window,' he adds. 'He disappeared into one of the inns across the street.' Asterix immediately asks *which* inn. 'Well, my memory might need jogging a bit,' the sailor answers slyly, seeing how desperate they are. 'Eleven gold coins should do the trick!'

If you have picked up the COINBAG during the adventure, use this to bribe the sailor for his information. Rotate the disc to 'count out' the 11 gold coins – then go to the number that appears on the other side of the card. If you don't have the COINBAG, go to 128 instead.

'Blue is right!' the farmer exclaims, throwing his arms round Asterix. 'So you are the great Asterix after all! I'll sketch you those faces straightaway.' But as he reaches inside his shirt for his sketchpad, the farmer suddenly becomes suspicious again. 'How do I know that you didn't just hear tell of that feat as well?' he asks guardedly, returning to his milking. 'How do I know that you're not just Romans in disguise? I'm going to give you another test to be absolutely sure about you. Asterix once went to help the famous Cleopatra in Egypt. What did she give him as a reward for his help – some precious manuscripts, a large diamond or a gold bangle from her wrist?' Again, Asterix can only scratch his head. All he can remember clearly about his meeting with Cleopatra is that she had a very pretty nose!

Which of the three options would you suggest Asterix answers?

If precious manuscripts	**go to 16**
If large diamond	**go to 98**
If gold bangle	**go to 184**

'You've got to give it to those Romans,' Asterix comments thoughtfully, a short while after he and Obelix most certainly *have* given it to them, having knocked them all unconscious! 'Their ambush strategy is quite brilliant. Did you see how they hid themselves where the path was at its absolute narrowest? It gave them the maximum advantage over us when they swept down from the hill.' Obelix scratches his head in confusion. 'But if they had the maximum advantage, Asterix,' he asks, 'how come we won?' It's now Asterix's turn to scratch his head. 'Yes, a good point,' he concedes. 'I hadn't really thought about that!' ***Go to 149.***

253

As the trio approach the bridge, however, they notice that there are two guard towers at the near end. They would have to pass straight between them! 'Remember, we're not meant to be fighting any more Romans than we absolutely have to,' Asterix remarks thoughtfully. 'So I'm afraid it's a bit of a dip for us! We'll swim directly *under* the bridge, between its supports, so the guards won't see us!' As soon as they have swum to the other end of the bridge, they creep up on to the bank and stealthily make their way into the town's narrow streets. ***Go to 147.***

254
THE GAULS
ARE CONFRONTED BY

ROMAN PATROLS HERE

Keep throwing the dice until the Gauls have knocked out this number of patrols. Any magic potions rolled before this total is reached must be deducted from the score on the MAGIC POTION COUNTER. When the Gauls have finished the fight, go to 281.

255

'Klunkklix *is* one of our number,' the man tells them, 'but not in Lutetia! The fact that you know the name proves that you must be Roman agents who have done a bit of investigating into our movement. Pity it wasn't quite investigating enough!' And, at that, he suddenly whips out a whistle from his pocket and gives it a short, sharp blow. Like magic, a number of muscular men appear from the crowd, starting to converge on the two Gauls. Asterix uncorks his gourd of magic potion in readiness for the confrontation but then decides it would be more prudent just to cut and run. As they dart from one street to another, however, he unfortunately spills some of his potion. He hadn't pushed the cork firmly enough into the gourd! 'What a waste!' he says with a sigh. 'I really must be more careful in future.'

Reduce MAGIC POTION by 1 measure. Go next to 96.

The Roman is only too happy to give Obelix an answer. '*Mañana* means tomorrow!' he snarls at him. 'Every true Spaniard knows that. So you're not Spaniards at all. And you're both under arrest!' Asterix and Obelix immediately take flight but the Roman is very fit (he once won a bronze medal in the CCCC metres at the Empire Games) and almost as fast as they are. It's a good twenty minutes before the Gauls have lost him and by then Asterix is panting for breath. He decides that he'd better take a measure of his magic potion for a quick recovery!

Reduce MAGIC POTION by 1 measure. Go next to 174.

'Where to next?' Obelix enquires of his friend as the trio now leave the streets of Camaracum. 'Is our *third* destination somewhere that specialises in wild boar?' he asks, still not giving up on the idea. Asterix shakes his head, though. 'No, the place we're heading for now is famous for its very fizzy wine,' he tells him. 'It's quite expensive and so people usually drink it only on very special occasions. The town is called Durocortorum.' Since Durocortorum isn't *too* many miles away – and they still have most of the day in front of them – Asterix wonders whether they should take the scenic route. Or would it be more sensible just to follow the main road again?

What will you decide for them?

If take the scenic route   **go to 10**
If keep to the main road   **go to 189**

258

'There's something wrong here,' Obelix remarks, bewildered, after he has collected all the helmets from the unconscious Romans. 'I've counted *fifty* helmets,' he says, 'but only *forty-nine* Romans. It doesn't make sense!' Knowing that his friend isn't exactly the world's best mathematician, Asterix starts to check his adding up. But his figures are exactly the same: *fifty* helmets and only *forty-nine* Romans. 'Ah, there's the explanation,' Asterix says, happening to glance up into the trees and spotting a Roman draped over the branches. 'One of the helmets must have become detached from the soldiers. Or should I say one of the soldiers must have become detached from the helmets!' *Go to 40*.

259
THE GAULS
ARE CONFRONTED BY

ROMAN PATROLS HERE

Keep throwing the dice until the Gauls have knocked out this number of patrols. Any magic potions rolled before this total is reached must be deducted from the score on the MAGIC POTION COUNTER. When the Gauls have finished the fight, go to 52.

260

The Romans were all packed in The Merry Ox's cellar again. But this time they weren't waiting to jump out, they were just . . . well . . . *out*! The cart-driver is horrified at the scene he has just witnessed and begins to fear for his own skin. As they resume their journey to Durocortorum, he prays that the Gauls don't suddenly realise *his* part in the ambush. But Asterix already has done. He'd been wondering for quite a while now why someone would be delivering a barrel of wine to a town *renowned* for its wine. But he decides that he might as well have the rest of the free ride first. Only when they have reached Durocortorum will he perhaps give the cart-driver a good thump! *Go to 137*.

The next stage of our heroes' journey is the longest: all the way down to Lugdunum. Since it's far too many miles for them to walk, they ask round to see if any long-distance carts are due to set off that way. They discover that two overnight post-carts – one first class and the other second class – will be departing for Lugdunum soon and so they decide to hide in the back of one of these. But which should they choose? The first class cart would be a lot faster (although some of the locals complained that it was often no faster than the second class one!) but the second class cart was perhaps less likely to be searched by a Roman patrol on the journey.

Which post-cart do you want them to choose?

| If first class cart | **go to 139** |
| If second class cart | **go to 194** |

'Sunstroke is correct,' the Roman exclaims with some surprise. 'And talking of sunstroke,' he continues, his manner immediately more friendly, 'you should be very careful with your pale skin. The sun can make you go very dopey. In fact, in the case of your fat friend there, it looks as if it might be too late for him already.' Obelix suddenly jumps up, about to thump the Roman, but he reluctantly sits down again on receiving a cautionary glance from Asterix. 'See? I was right,' the Roman exclaims before walking off. 'The sun is making him act very strangely already!' *Go to 241.*

Our heroes finally reach their village – and, indeed, it is as heroes they are greeted. The whole population, from Chief Vitalstatistix to youngest child, comes out to cheer them. 'We knew you would make it, Asterix and Obelix!' the chief cries joyfully, throwing his arms round them. 'We were so confident that we've even got the table already set for the banquet. All we have to do now is invite that smug centurion to our feast of regional specialities. Just as we warned him before you set off on your mission, though . . . the only thing he'll be eating is a huge humble pie!'

Well done! Your skill has enabled Asterix to complete his long journey and win the wager with the centurion. Don't forget, though, that the real objective of the game is to make him complete the journey with as little magic potion drunk as possible. Unless you have a final score of 8 on the MAGIC POTION COUNTER, why not try again and see if you can improve upon your result?

'So we did apprehend the right Asterix!' the captain says after he has told the real Asterix that his password is wrong. 'Put him in chains, men!' While the Romans are manacling the snivelling thief, Asterix realises that there is only one thing for it. If the Romans will absolutely insist that the thief is Asterix, then he'll just have to help him *act* like Asterix. 'Just hold the wretch's nose a moment will you, Obelix?' Asterix says as he uncorks his gourd of magic potion. He then pours a measure down the thief's throat. 'Yes, he certainly seems a lot more like me now!' Asterix chuckles as he and Obelix grab their bag and make a run for it. 'I'm sure those flying Romans think so too!'

Reduce MAGIC POTION by 1 measure. Go next to 48.

265

It looks as if our heroes are going to get away with it because the Romans eventually prepare to leave the ship again. But then the centurion suddenly spots Asterix's bright red trousers! 'Hey, YOU!' the centurion calls out to Asterix. 'How come you're not wearing the sailor's customary blue and white striped breeches? Take a look at that fat oaf standing next to you. *That's* what genuine sailor's breeches look like! So what do you have to say for yourself?' **Go to 83.**

'Fingerlix? No, of course Fingerlix isn't my name,' the waiter replies in a most irritated manner. 'Don't you think I'm quite busy enough without being bothered by people trying to guess my name for some stupid reason? And stop hogging that vinegar, will you. Can't you see that the customer behind wants it for his salad?' In actual fact, it isn't vinegar next to Asterix's plate – but his gourd of precious magic potion. Before Asterix can stop him, though, the waiter has reached forwards, grabbed the gourd, and handed it to the customer sitting at the table behind. He only returns it to Asterix when that unsuspecting person has given his food a very liberal sprinkle with the potion. Asterix dreads to think of the effect that it will have. Even boar vindaloo wouldn't have that strength!

Reduce MAGIC POTION by 1 measure. Go next to 168.

267
THE GAULS
ARE CONFRONTED BY

ROMAN PATROLS HERE

Keep throwing the dice until the Gauls have knocked out this number of patrols. Any magic potions rolled before this total is reached must be deducted from the score on the MAGIC POTION COUNTER. When the Gauls have finished the fight, go to 130.

'All down!' Obelix exclaims with satisfaction as he surveys the dazed bodies strewn about him. 'No, they're not. There's just one left and he's sneaking away!' He's about to give chase to this Roman but Asterix holds him back. 'You'll never find your way back to us in this maze,' he warns him. 'I think you'd better let him go!' Obelix might be deterred by this warning – but Dogmatix certainly isn't. He immediately scampers off in pursuit of the Roman. 'That's the last I'll ever see of him!' Obelix sobs – but a few minutes later Dogmatix has returned to them. With a large piece of a soldier's tunic between his teeth! *Go to 218*.

269

'Two roast boar and an amphora of goats' milk, please,' Asterix says casually to the amazed innkeeper after they have laid out all the Romans. The innkeeper can't move, though. He still can't believe what he's just seen. This puny little man and his unfit-looking friend just knocked out *nine* Roman patrols! 'S-s-sorry,' he speaks eventually. 'Could you say that order again? Nine roast patrols, was it, and an amphora of black eyes?' Asterix can't understand what's wrong with the innkeeper. He seems for some reason to be in a state of shock! *Go to 149*.

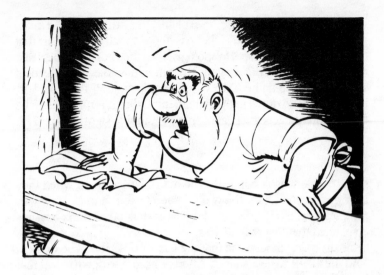

270

Yes, Asterix most certainly *can* see the bag! It's being carried by a wretched-looking creature who is running for all he's worth away from the quay and into the town. He must have been hiding on one of the other ships but decided to make a run for it when he saw the Gauls board *this* ship. 'Quick, after him!' Asterix yells and the trio are soon charging along the quay themselves. But the thief again seems to vanish into thin air! 'He has to be in one of those three inns over there,' Asterix exclaims. 'Either The Skull and Crossbones, The Wooden Leg or The Cutlass and Parrot!'

Which inn do you want them to enter?

If The Skull and Crossbones   **go to 108**
If The Wooden Leg   **go to 250**
If The Cutlass and Parrot   **go to 69**

271

'I'm sorry I couldn't warn you lads about them Romans,' the boat's captain apologises to Asterix and Obelix after the three patrols have been sent flying over the side into the water. 'If I didn't let them hide in me empty apple barrels,' he explains, 'they threatened to make me walk me own plank!' Obelix is about to tell the captain that there's absolutely no need to apologise, but then he remembers that they're meant to be *avoiding* the Romans if possible. So as the boat sets sail for Lutetia he has a wistful last look at all those soldiers bobbing up and down in the water behind them. It might be some time before he gets a repeat of that pleasurable sight! ***Go to 102.***

272

'No, my name isn't Sandkix!' the man snaps at them when they have approached him. 'Now if you don't want sand kicks *in your face*, scarper!' As the disconsolate Gauls walk off, Asterix remains convinced that that *was* the Resistance leader. 'He had exactly the same drooping moustache that the farmer described,' he broods, 'and the identical nose shape!' Asterix's head is so down in fact that he walks right into a child's sand citadel (the ancient equivalent of a sand-castle). As he tumbles over it, the cork comes out of his magic potion gourd and some of the potion leaks away.

Reduce MAGIC POTION by 1 measure. Go next to 241.

273
THE GAULS
ARE CONFRONTED BY

ROMAN PATROLS HERE

Keep throwing the dice until the Gauls have knocked out this number of patrols. Any magic potions rolled before this total is reached must be deducted from the score on the MAGIC POTION COUNTER. When the Gauls have finished the fight, go to 32.

274

'Hurry up, Obelix, back in the chariot!' Asterix calls to him urgently when the Romans have been knocked all over the road. 'We don't want to have to fight those soldiers from the roadblock in the other lane as well. Look, they're coming towards us right now!' As a matter of fact, Obelix *did* want to have to fight these soldiers as well . . . but Asterix yanks him into the chariot and gives a sharp jerk on the horse's reins. Surprisingly, the weary horse is able to outpace the Romans. Asterix rather suspects, though, that this is because the petrified Romans are chasing *slowly* not because their horse is moving *quickly!'* ***Go to 101.***

275

'I hope you'll be paying for all this damage!' the innkeeper rages at Asterix after the Romans have all been sent crashing into the tables or flying over the bar. He quickly falls silent, though, as Asterix now menacingly advances on *him*. 'Well, if you'd had the courage to shout out to us as we stepped through your door,' he addresses him sternly, 'and *warned* us that there were loads of Romans drinking in here, then all this could have been avoided!' Our three friends are about to leave when Asterix remembers why they had come to the inn in the first place. He demands to know which boat can be trusted to give them a safe passage to Lutetia. Keen to get them well away from the town, the innkeeper is only too eager to provide this information! *Go to 102*.

276

When the shopkeeper tells him that Freekix is wrong, Asterix tries to have another guess. But the shopkeeper spots the little gourd at Asterix's belt before he can get the name out. 'I bet there's hemlock in there to poison all my sweets, isn't there, Roman spy?' he screams at him, snatching the gourd from him and starting to pour the potion on to the floor. Although Asterix manages to grab it back again, it's not before a good measure's worth of the potion has been spilt.

Reduce MAGIC POTION by 1 measure. Go next to 257.

277

While the Gauls are buying a pot of fish stew from the skinny dark-haired woman, Dogmatix suddenly scampers off. 'Where's he gone this time?' Asterix says, tutting, as they walk round the harbour looking for him. Suddenly, he hears a familiar yapping coming from one of the many small rowing-boats there. 'Now what are you doing in that poor man's boat?' Asterix chides him as Dogmatix leaps out to join them again. But then Asterix has a closer look at the man . . . ***Go to 175.***

278

'Hold-up is wrong!' the Roman bawls at Asterix, jabbing him in his ribs. 'So this *is* a hold-up! Hands on your heads and walk slowly towards my chariot outside. I'm taking you both in!' But there are now so many chariots and ox carts parked outside that the Roman can't work out which one is his! 'Now where did I park it?' he asks, removing his helmet to scratch his head. While he is trying to remember, our heroes quietly slip away to their *own* chariot. 'I'd be laughing even louder,' Asterix chuckles, holding his sides, 'if I hadn't secretly swigged some magic potion while he was scratching his head. I thought I might be needing it . . . but what a waste!'

Reduce MAGIC POTION by 1 measure. ***Go next to 168.***

279

'Yes, I'm Nosepix. And you must be the two famous outlaws the Romans are looking for?' the bowls player says, immediately shaking Asterix by the hand. 'Now what can my Resistance unit do to help you in your mission?' he adds. 'Provide money? Disguises? False papers?' It's at that moment that Asterix happens to glance towards the far end of the quay. 'Well, in actual fact there's something you can do to help us this very moment,' he says. 'We're getting a little behind schedule, you see . . . and there's a large contingent of Romans coming in this direction!' *Go to 115*.

280
THE GAULS
ARE CONFRONTED BY

ROMAN PATROLS HERE

Keep throwing the dice until the Gauls have knocked out this

number of patrols. Any magic potions rolled before this total is reached must be deducted from the score on the MAGIC POTION COUNTER. When the Gauls have finished the fight, go to 233.

281

'The water's absolutely freezing, isn't it?' Asterix calls out to all the dazed Romans as they bob up and down below them. 'I don't know what it's like for you,' he adds with a snigger, 'but when I was in the water a few minutes ago, my teeth were chattering. Thanks to you, though, I feel a lot warmer now. It's amazing what a little bit of brisk exercise can do!' In fact, Asterix is wondering whether he should indulge in a bit more *brisk exercise*. Cowering behind some cider barrels is the boat's captain, who had obviously taken a bribe from the Romans to let them hide on his boat. But Asterix resists the temptation to toss him into the water as well. They're going to need the wretch to sail the boat to Lutetia for them! ***Go to 102***.

282

The cart-driver stands at the door of The Crushed Grape unable to believe his eyes. The Crushed Roman would be more appropriate! 'Look out – it's a trap!' he yells, hoping that the Gauls won't realise how belated the warning is. 'There are loads of Romans coming up from the cellar!' Obelix is still in such a state of euphoria from the fight that he genuinely thanks the cart-driver for his warning. Asterix, though, has guessed about his role in the ambush. If it wasn't for the fact that the wretch would be useful to transport them the rest of the way to Durocortorum, he would have given him a warning back. And that one would be well after the event too! *Go to 137*.

283

'There seems to be a roadblock ahead,' Asterix observes anxiously. 'The Romans must be on the lookout for someone. A denarius to a sestertius that it's *us* and that stolen chariot!' So they decide that they had better leave the road and walk cross-country the rest of the way to Camaracum, following one of two rough tracks nearby. But the Romans have anticipated this possibility and placed an ambush at the first bend of each track!

Which of the two tracks do you want the Gauls to take?

If the narrower one   **go to 132**
If the wider one   **go to 213**

Since they don't have that sort of money, Obelix just has to put all the food back again. Dejected, he goes back down the counter, replacing each platter of boar over its appropriate candle (for keeping it warm). 'Never mind,' Asterix consoles him as they sit down with all that they *could* afford: two small tankards of goats' milk. 'I'll give Dogmatix a little of my magic potion,' he says, 'and he can go and *hunt* some boar for us while we're sipping our drinks. He could probably do with some exercise . . . and free-range boar is so much nicer than this tasteless processed sort, anyway!'

Reduce MAGIC POTION by 1 measure. Go next to 168.

285

The shopkeeper suddenly draws much nearer to the Gauls, furtively glancing all about him. 'Ah, so you two are the go-betweens?' he whispers. 'The ones who have come to collect the bag of gold coins we have scraped together and deliver it to the freedom fighters hiding in the forests?' Asterix and Obelix can only blink in confusion. 'We are?' Asterix asks, bewildered. 'Well, at least, I *thought* you were the ones,' the shopkeeper says, starting to have doubts about them. 'You certainly gave me the correct code. But perhaps it was just a coincidence that you chose *green and red humbugs*. I'd better make sure with a second check. Would you like your green and red humbugs in a basket, a pot or a box?'

Which do you want them to choose?

If basket	**go to 106**
If pot	**go to 70**
If box	**go to 192**

'Congratulations! You're my hundredth customer this week,' the shopkeeper greets them as they enter his premises. 'That means you get two bottles of fizzy wine free!' Obelix is delighted by this but Asterix can't take his eyes off the shopkeeper's nose. It's an even

brighter red than his awning outside! Didn't that farmer tell them that the Resistance leader here had a very red nose? Asterix desperately tries to remember the name they were given. It would prove to the shopkeeper that they could be trusted. Now was it Nosepix, Freekix or Chokkybix?

If you have picked up the SKETCHPAD during the adventure, you may consult it here to find out the shopkeeper's name. If not, you'll have to guess which of the three possibilities Asterix should give.

If you prefer NOSEPIX	**go to 9**
If you prefer FREEKIX	**go to 124**
If you prefer CHOKKYBIX	**go to 67**

JUST AS I THOUGHT!

287

'Just as I thought!' the centurion barks, approaching right up to Asterix's nose. 'You're not a sailor at all!' Obelix gives the centurion a gentle tap on the shoulder. 'Oh, nor am I by the way,' he tells him casually, 'and I'm not FAT either!' The centurion's brief distraction gives Asterix time to have a quick swig of his magic potion. But there are far too many Romans to fight on this occasion and so Asterix simply jumps overboard. Obelix and Dogmatix immediately follow him. 'The voyage was nearly over anyway,' Asterix says as they speed through the water. 'And this is far less strenuous than swabbing decks!'

Reduce MAGIC POTION by 1 measure. Go next to 217.

288

Obelix tells Asterix to calm down, though. All this stress is not good for him! 'Let's pull in at that service inn ahead,' he suggests, 'and you can have a nice relaxing tankard of goats' milk.' When they've parked their cart at the service inn they find that they have a choice of three places where they can eat: the waiter-service area, the self-service area and the boar-burger bar.

Which will you choose for them?

If waiter-service area	**go to 127**
If self-service area	**go to 90**
If boar-burger bar	**go to 45**

THE GAULS
ARE CONFRONTED BY

ROMAN PATROLS HERE

Keep throwing the dice until the Gauls have knocked out this number of patrols. Any magic potions rolled before this total is reached must be deducted from the score on the MAGIC POTION COUNTER. When the Gauls have finished the fight, go to 220.

Other exciting titles in the Hodder and Stoughton Adventure Game Books series are:

For Younger Readers:

FAMOUS FIVE ADVENTURE GAMES:

THE WRECKERS' TOWER GAME
THE HAUNTED RAILWAY GAME
THE WHISPERING ISLAND GAME
THE SINISTER LAKE GAME
THE WAILING LIGHTHOUSE GAME
THE SECRET AIRFIELD GAME
THE SHUDDERING MOUNTAIN GAME
THE MISSING SCIENTIST GAME

ASTERIX ADVENTURE GAMES:

ASTERIX TO THE RESCUE
OPERATION BRITAIN

THE PETER PAN ADVENTURE GAME:

PETER'S REVENGE

BIGGLES ADVENTURE GAMES:

THE SECRET NIGHT FLYER GAME
THE HIDDEN BLUEPRINTS GAME

GHOST ADVENTURE GAMES:

GHOSTLY TOWERS
GHOST TRAIN

For Older Readers:

THE FOOTBALL ADVENTURE GAME:

TACTICS!

WHO-DONE-IT ADVENTURE GAME:

SUSPECTS!

BATTLE QUEST ADVENTURE GAME:

CAVES OF FURY
TUNNELS OF FEAR